Replaceable You Are

A Chi-Town Love Story

A NOVEL BY

TNESHA SIMS

ACKNOWLEDGMENTS

I have to take a moment and acknowledge my Royalty family; the support and the everyday encouragement keeps me motivated. Porscha Sterling, thank you for giving me the opportunity to be a part of this wonderful team.

To my family and friends, thank you for the continuous support. I love you all so much. Thank you for being patient and understanding. I know I have been distant, but the reason behind it is worth it.

Tone, I will continue to write so that you have something to read. I pray and believe that God will bring you home to us safely. Keep your faith, brother, and know that we are all behind you. We love you so much.

To my wonderful co-worker, thank you for being not only the best social worker at our company but my personal counselor at times. You don't know how much you make my job easier.

FOLLOW ME ON SOCIAL MEDIA:

Instagram: @authortneshasims

Facebook: Tnesha Sims

Chanel

"*W*here are the keys to the car?" Jamel yelled. I rolled my eyes under the covers. Somehow, I knew he was going to ask that. He does it every damn morning.

"The keys are in my purse, Mel!" I yelled back. See, Jamel and I were high school sweethearts, and we've been together seven years. We weren't the perfect couple by far, but we were a good looking couple. At times, I felt like I couldn't live without him. Then, there were times I couldn't believe I was still around. Somewhere along the way, Jamel didn't seem like he was really trying to move forward with our relationship. He was okay with what was current, and I was slowly feeling distant.

"Okay, baby," Mel whispered as he kissed my forehead. "I'm taking RJ to the blood bank." I pulled the covers completely off my head and sat in an upright position.

"You know RJ goes to that damn blood bank as if that's his job," I said with a little attitude.

"Chill out, Nel," he said. Jamel and everyone else I'm close with calls me Nel, but my whole name is Chanel Renae Booker. Mel's real name is Jamel Lee Jones, Jr.

"I'm not starting anything. RJ needs to get a real job and quit

1

depending on my sister to take care of him. And you riding out the gas that I put in my car is getting a little old."

"Okay, Nel. I can take a hint, and I'll have your tank back on full as always, baby," Mel said in his sexy voice.

Mel left me in bed as he does every Friday morning to be with his boys. I worked at Licensed Professional Counseling Clinic making damn good money, and I was currently on vacation for two weeks. Although I loved my job as a victim's advocate, I actually wanted to be a therapist. There is room for me to grow after graduating, but until then, I'm rolling with the punches for the money.

In six months, your girl will have her Master's degree in Clinical Mental Health Counseling. Jamel works at a label company where he helps produce, mix beats, and write short lyrics for a number of artists. He makes pretty decent money. It's really a front to cover up being a drug dealer, which is where most of his money comes from.

I'm looking to better myself because I refuse to work in an office under someone else for the rest of my life or depend on Mel, although he gives me the world. Don't get me wrong it's a great job, but without a degree I can't move up the ladder and become someone else's boss. Plus, I would struggle on my own if something were to happen to Mel. I want to own my own clinic where I can counsel people. As for Jamel, it seems like the street life is as good as it's going to get with him. I wish he would turn the money into legit money.

Jamel likes to run the streets with my sister Angie's boyfriend, RJ, and our homeboy, Money. I knew Money before Mel. Money actually introduced us. As for RJ, I don't think he will ever get his shit together.

He lost his mom, and he used that as an excuse to lie around and do nothing.

I reached over to grab my cell phone off the nightstand to see that I had four missed calls; two from my sister and two from my girl, Da'Sha, who I also call Sha. I knew what my sister wanted, and it was the weekend so I could only imagine what Sha wanted.

I dragged myself out of bed to shower, so I could get my day started. After my shower, I cooked myself some eggs, bacon, and oatmeal. I cleaned our crib the day before so I wouldn't have to today. I grabbed my cell phone and sat on my fluffy couch. I called my sister back, and she answered on the first ring.

"Hey, sis," I said as sweet as ever.

"Hey, girl. I called you to see what plans you got going on this weekend," she stated.

"Well, I don't know yet, but Da'Sha called me, so I know she got some shit on the floor."

"Okay. Well, hit Sha up and call me back because I need some excitement tonight, and I need a break from RJ's ass. RJ is just a—"

"Bum ass nigga," I interrupted her.

"Yes," Angie agreed. I hung up with her and called Sha up.

"Damn, bitch. It took you forever to call me back!" Sha yelled soon as she picked up the phone.

"Well, hello to you too, friend," I laughed.

She laughed and told me how the club was going to be jumping this weekend and about the car shows that were going on also. She asked if I wanted to go to the mall and, of course, I told her yeah. After I hung up with Sha, I called Angie back and told her to get ready because we're on our way to the mall to shop.

The mall wasn't as packed as it usually would be on a Friday, which was a good thing because there was always some shit going down at the mall on Fridays like fights, stealing, and whatever else the ratchet folks would bring to our mall. As we were walking past Footlocker, a promoter ran up to Sha and gave her a flyer for the club tonight and asked her to bring her friends. Of course, she told him we would all be there. We grabbed a few more things, and I grabbed Jamel a few Polo shirts, pants, and a few pairs of Rock jeans before we left.

In the car it was unusually quiet, so I broke the ice. "So what's been good, sis? You and RJ ok?"

"Girl, are we ever? Some days I just want to tell him to pack his shit and leave. I wish he would just get it together."

I turned around and faced Angie. "Is it that bad now?"

"It's been that bad," she stated with tears in her eyes. I knew she was serious this time around because my sis and RJ had a lot of issues, but she never talked the way she was talking now. I didn't want to bring her spirit down, so I changed the subject.

"Well, let's go out and have a great time. Let's see what Chicago has to offer," I said while dancing in my seat and making them both laugh.

"Yea, I'm about to have a good time and show out tonight," Angie laughed. Sha dropped us off at our homes, and we went our separate ways for the time being.

Jamel

"Man, what you got planned tonight?" RJ asked me, playing Call of Duty on Money's sofa.

"Shit, man, I really don't know," I said, sitting next to RJ.

"Your ass knows you about to be laid up with Nel's ass, nigga," Money joked.

"Man, yeah right. I ain't trying to be in that girl's face tonight. Besides, I'm trying to get up with Candy's sexy, redbone ass," I said as I licked my full, sexy lips.

"Man, you got a bad bitch at home. Why the fuck would you want to mess that up? Y'all niggas trip me out," Money shook his head at me.

"What, nigga? You got a bad bitch in your shit every other night. What the fuck you mean?" I said, getting irritated with the conversation already.

"Man, and that's me, but on the real if one of them was halfway on the level Nel is...trust me...I wouldn't. When I find a nice one like Nel, I just might settle down. Until then, I'm doing me. Besides, these hoes are only around for my paper. Every bitch wants a thug in their life, but only a real woman can tame one," Money said, hitting the button on the controller repeatedly and trying his best to stay up with the game.

"Whatever. Nel okay and all, but she got her flaws. Trust me, I know," I said patiently waiting for my turn to beat RJ.

"Yo, on the real, how can you fix your mouth and say some shit like that about your wifey? Or is she still wifey?" Money asked.

"Hell yeah, that's my baby, but I ain't trying to wife her no time soon. A nigga only twenty-seven and trying to get this paper. She's twenty-five and almost done with school. We got ten years for that to even be thought of. As a matter of fact, why you sweating my bitch? You want her, nigga?" I joked but really wanted to know.

"Yeah, okay, nigga. Nel would leave your ass high and dry if I tried to holla at her," Money joked.

"Fuck you, bitch ass nigga," I said with a little too much bass in my voice for Money.

"Nigga, you were serious?" Money asked, putting the game on hold.

I shrugged. "When it comes to my bitch, yes, nigga."

"Okay, man, y'all tripping for real." RJ finally jumped in the conversation.

"Naw, this nigga tripping over my bitch, though," I yelled.

"Nigga, Nel is like a lil' sis to me. I'm the one that introduced her to your ass right before I was about to skip math class in high school. So what the fuck you mean, nigga?" Money said, standing up.

I looked at RJ, and we both burst out laughing. "Man, only your ass would remember skipping a class in high school," RJ laughed.

"Man, shut up. But on the real, nigga, I'm just trying to tell you to

6

appreciate what you have at home," Money stated calmly.

"Man, we good, though," I said.

"Okay. Can we get back to this game, or are y'all some pussy ass niggas?" RJ laughed.

"Man, don't get me started on you about Angie," Money smiled, showing his perfect set of white teeth.

"That's why I'm not going to get you started," RJ laughed at Money.

Nel

$\mathcal{I}$ was sitting on my daybed staring out of my window. I only had six more months, and I would be graduating with my Master's in Clinical Mental Health Counseling. I decided to take my last few classes online, except for one class that I have on campus at the University of Illinois. It would be great because I wouldn't have a lot to do before I walk across that stage. My girl, Sha and I have been at this college thing for four years taking a shit load of classes to get finished. We're more than ready to be finished.

I was hesitant on whether to call Mel or not since he hasn't called me all day. I missed him calling and checking in on me. I grabbed my cell and hit speed dial.

"What up?" Mel spoke into the phone.

"What I tell you about that? I'm not one of your homeboys that you be talking to," I said, wishing I never called his ass.

"Man, like I said…what's up? I'm assuming you called me for a reason," he sighed.

"Yeah, I miss you. You haven't called me all day. What's up with that?" I said with a little attitude coming on.

"Man, I've been a lil' busy, Nel," he breathed into the phone.

"Man, that nigga been sitting on his ass all day, Nel. Don't believe that shit." I heard Money say in the background.

"Oh, is that right, Jamel?" I laughed, but my feelings were hurt at the same time.

"Man, this hating ass nigga… Don't listen to him, baby. I miss you too," Mel confessed.

I smiled at his confession that he missed me.

"So, what you got planned tonight, baby?" Mel asked.

"Mm, me and the girls are going out tonight unless you want to do something. What about dinner and a movie?" I asked, getting excited.

"Naw, maybe tomorrow, baby. Ok?" he said.

"Oh, okay, Mel. Well, I'll talk to you whenever I see you later tonight," I said with disappointment in my voice as I hung up. I was hurt, but Mel turned down wanting to spend time together so often that I should be used to it by now. Love and history will have you doing some crazy things.

It was 6:30 pm, and I wanted to bathe and take a quick nap before my night out with the girls. I was getting up to grab a glass of wine when my phone rang.

"Hello?" I said, thinking it was probably my sis or Sha.

"You mad at daddy?" Mel spoke through the phone.

I had to look at the phone to make sure it was really him. He never called me back after I hung up on him. He usually talked to me when he got home about me hanging up in his face.

"Well, my feelings are a little hurt, but I'll get over it as I always do," I said softly.

He chuckled before he spoke.

"Nel, you know I love you, girl. As a matter of fact, I'll take you out tomorrow around eight for dinner. Okay, baby?" he said in his sexy voice.

"Okay," I said a little shocked.

"Okay, see you later after you leave the club, baby," he mentioned.

"Okay, baby. I love you," I said in my baby voice.

"You know I like that voice… gon' get a nigga all hard and shit, Nel," Mel joked.

It wasn't that Mel wasn't in love with me—he was. I meant more to him than anyone, but he just let the street life get the best of him. Besides, who wouldn't like a five-feet-five, brown eyed, peanut butter smooth skin, 38C breasts, small waist and nice ass having chick like myself? I kept my hair done, it was so thick and healthy. I had a beautiful, round face and a smile females would kill for. Guys tried to holla at me left and right, but I was committed to Mel.

Mel was six feet even with a dark skin complexion. He was clean cut. He had just cut his dreads off, which gave him a sexier look. He had nice, white teeth and a dimple on the left side of his face. He was muscular and worked hard to keep his appearance up. When people said we were a cute couple, it was more than true. People tested our relationship all the time. I never fed into it, but Mel somehow got caught up in the shit. If he had any sidelines he must be doing a damn good job at keeping them in check because I haven't heard of him doing anything out here in the streets, as far as she goes.

"Well, if you come home I could give you something before I get ready for tonight," I said in my sexiest voice for Mel.

"Damn, bae. Give me about fifteen minutes. You got my shit rock hard 'round these niggas," Mel laughed as we hung up.

****

I was getting myself ready for Mel when he walked into the house.

"What's under that robe, baby? I hope it's something for me?" he said, walking toward me.

"You'll find out, Mr. Jones," I cooed. I wrapped my arms around his neck, kissing him with so much passion while he squeezed my ass.

"Damn, girl, I want you right here," Mel said, fondling my breasts.

"Take it then, baby," was all I could say in response.

He laid me down on our loveseat and started to slowly kiss down my body toward my belly button. He licked my belly button and kissed down by my pelvis, making his way to my thighs.

"Umm, baby, yes… it feels so good," I whispered.

Finally, he dove right into my pussy. He went to work sucking, licking, flicking his tongue, and making me cum right away.

"Oh, I'm not done yet, baby," he said, flipping me over on my stomach before shoving his thick, eight inches inside me.

All you could hear were moans and groans as we made love for about two hours. I swear this man was irreplaceable.

"Take a shower with me?" he asked after wrapping me up in his arms.

"I was gonna take a hot bath, but I guess I can make that happen," I said. Of course, the shower was round two, and we made love all over again.

Angie

As I was preparing for the club tonight, the job offer I recently received from a law firm crossed my mind. I wanted to take it, but I also loved working for my current firm. I knew taking the offer would only mean that I would have to work just as hard to make partner at their firm. Maybe it wasn't worth it right now. I walked to my closet and got my clothes out for the night. I laid out my black dress with my red, Gucci heels and matching clutch.

I'm Nel's older sister, and you can best believe what they say about the older the better, you age like fine wine, because I have hips and ass for days. My breasts were a perfect size and my flat stomach— Lord, I shut shit down. I'm a little darker than Nel, though. My skin has a golden brown glow. I have a shortcut that complemented my hazel eyes. My sister, Sha, and I together turn more than heads. We turn necks, shoulders, backs, and every other body part that could turn on a male and female.

Sha was a sexy redbone. She was thick with long, jet-black hair that she kept in a bun, brown eyes, and big, sexy, red lips. She had a three-year-old son, who was staying with his dad in Michigan until school starts.

I started to run a hot bath when RJ came into the room.

"Damn, nigga, you walking in all quiet. You scared the shit out of me. Who dropped you off? Mel?" I asked.

"Naw, my man, Money," he said, looking on the bed at my outfit.

"You wearing that little ass dress tonight, and you didn't ask my permission about going out, did you?"

I had to do a double-take at his ass.

"Nigga, first off, don't come in my house with that bullshit. When you start buying my clothes...hell, even your own damn clothes...I might listen to your ass. And I don't have to ask your ass to do shit. I pay all these damn bills, go to work every day, cook, and clean while your ass run the streets with the money I give your ass. So gon' on with that shit."

RJ turned around and said, "Fuck you."

Then he walked right back out the door.

RJ

I was beyond pissed. *Even though Angie paid all the bills and still was able to keep my pockets fat, it doesn't give her the right to disrespect me.* I thought to myself. I decided to take a walk to the park across the street from our house and watch the young fellows play ball. I really wanted to be a rapper and to be honest; I was actually good at the shit. I just blew a lot of opportunities that presented themselves to me. Like, my boy, Mel, could help me pursue my dreams, but Angie called that shit a *little hobby*. Sometimes, I can't stand her big booty ass.

My phone began to ring, so I took it out of my pocket to answer.

"Yo', who this?"

"That's how you answer for wifey?"

Sherry? This pretty young thang has been blowing my damn phone up.

"Man, I told your ass to stop calling me. I got a wife, and you ain't my bitch," I yelled. I was tired of this bitch calling and texting me.

"That ain't what your ass said a few weeks ago when you woke up in my pussy, nigga," Sherry said to me with an attitude.

"Bitch, please! I was fucked up that night. Your ass was a one-night stand, so stop calling me, you thirsty bitch."

I was about to hang up, but she hung up first. I could block her number, but she would only call from someone else's phone. I knew I needed to change my number before Angie found out.

I was at a hotel party with Money, Dirty, Cruz, Mel and their boy, Biggie. I rode with Mel, but Mel snuck off to the next room with some thirsty chick and wouldn't answer the door or his phone. Everyone had a chick in their face, and I was stuck with no ride home at two o'clock in the morning.

I considered calling Angie, but that would mean putting Mel in a situation about not being able to drive me home, and then Angie would ask a million questions about where Mel was and mention the shit to Nel. I couldn't do that to my boy, so I went to the front desk and got a room. Before I headed to my room, I sat at the bar and ordered two Hennessey and cokes. I wasn't feeling my drink like I wanted to, so I ordered a double shot on the rocks. I guess that third one did it because I was most definitely feeling it.

I stumbled to my room when I bumped into a PYT. She was thick as hell and had sexy, full lips. I told shorty my bad for bumping into her. She was looking at me like she wanted to rip my clothes off.

"It's okay, baby. I don't mind sexy, chocolate men bumping into me. Are you Future's lil' brother by any chance?" she smiled, biting down on her lips.

"Naw, but people say we favor. I'm RJ," I said, feeling a little dizzy.

"Um, RJ, you okay there?" she asked, trying to balance me against the wall I was leaning on.

"Yeah, I'm cool. I better get to my room before I pass out in this

hallway. Nice meeting you," I mumbled.

"Well, my name is Sherry. Let me help you to your room. What's your room number?" she asked, holding me up at the same time.

"I'm in room 409," I mumbled again.

"Give me your key so I can open the door," she said, reaching for the key.

She walked me into the bedroom and helped me out of my clothes. I thought she smelled hella good. Man, I was really wasted.

"Do you want me to stay and take care of you, baby?" she asked in the most seductive voice.

"I don't care," was all my crazy ass said before I passed out.

I managed to open my eyes thirty minutes later. Although my vision was blurred, I felt warm lips on my rock hard dick.

"Damn, girl. You know that shit drives me crazy," I said, getting the strength to lift up who I thought was Angie and sit her on my dick.

She started out slow. Angie's pussy is never this loose. I thought to myself, but it was juicy and wet so I dismissed the thought. It was seven o'clock when I finally opened my eyes and looked into the face of an unknown woman.

"What the fuck? Who the hell are you, and where is Angie?" I jumped up and asked.

"Sorry, I don't know who Angie is, baby, but she called you fifteen times already," she said, smiling.

"Man, what the fuck?" I said while grabbing my damn clothes and phone. I looked at my phone and called Mel.

"What up?" Mel answered.

"Man, where the fuck you at, nigga?" I yelled into the phone.

"Man, room 603," Mel said and hung up.

I know he had to been wondering what the fuck I was doing all damn night. He'd been trying to call my ass all night and into the morning. I was glad he hadn't left me. I knew he couldn't anyway; it would be too many questions to answer from our women.

I made it to Mel's room. I knocked on his door and waited for him to answer.

"Damn, nigga, where the fuck you been?" Mel asked, looking me at half dressed.

"Nigga, your ass was up in here fucking these hoes and didn't answer your damn phone last night, and I couldn't go home or call Angie without her asking me questions about you not bringing me home, nigga," I said all in one breath.

"So, I took my ass to the bar, got fucked up, and got fucked by this thirsty bitch that I don't even know." I was pissed off.

"Damn, man. I never thought your ass would get off that high horse and fuck around on Angie," Mel laughed while opening the door for Money.

"Man, I didn't even know it was even another bitch until I woke up. I was drunk as fuck last night with my dick in shorty's mouth, but I thought it was Angie, man. Damn," I said, hitting the wall with my fist.

"Man, calm down. What's done is done. We got to think about what we gon' tell these women of ours when we get back home," Mel said, *shaking his head.*

He never stayed out this late. He always made it home to Nel no later than four in the morning. He mentioned that he was also scared because Nel had called him twice, which meant she was waiting for his ass.

"Okay, okay, let me help y'all niggas out," Money laughed. "Tell them y'all went to the casino, got fucked up, and y'all hit big. Y'all passed out and your boy, Money, got y'all a room to keep y'all safe," he laughed at himself, trying to make himself the innocent one in the situation.

"Man, I guess that's all we got," Mel laughed, scared out his mind.

"Man, y'all niggas look shook," Money joked.

"Shit, I am." Mel and I both laughed but we were serious.

That shit was crazy, I thought to myself, still sitting on the bench at the park. It worked because the girls fell for it. Mel's ass had to drop two stacks for Nel to believe it. Money loaned me five stacks which I gave three of the five to Angie. She took that shit and ain't ask another question.

Now, all I had to do was change my number before I had to kill that Sherry bitch. She kept sending pictures, texts, and everything to my phone. I showed Mel and Money, and they told me to keep her sexy ass on the low, but fuck that. I got one girl, and I would lose her if I didn't get my shit together.

Sha

"*M*ommy misses you too, big boy," I said to my son on the phone. "I'll be there in a few weeks to get you, baby."

Benz got on the phone.

"Go play in your room, lil' man. Let me holla at your momma for a minute." I heard Benz say.

"Sha, baby, so what's going on? How you been?" Benz asked, trying to sound sexy.

"I've been good. I finally got my graduation package, and I'll be graduating in six months with my girl, Nel," I said excitedly.

"That's what up. I'm proud of you, baby girl. So, can we talk about my son coming to live with me for good?"

"Benz, we talked about this. Get your life together first," I said with irritation in my voice.

Benz asked many times could he get our son for good, but I wasn't about to let my son grow up around drugs. Benz was a big time drug dealer which is one reason why I left his ass. Benz let that lifestyle control him. Once he got the power, then came the fame along with the money and, of course, the bitches. He didn't know what to do with it. Being locked up twice and shot in the back should've slowed his ass down. No, it actually gave him more power, a faster life, and more money than he knew what to do with.

Each week he put $5,500 into my account for our son. Now, who couldn't live off that amount of money? That's $22,000 a month. I didn't let it change me, though. Although, it didn't stop me from buying a 2017 all-black Bentley with black-on-black rims that Benz helped me pick out. I also had an all-white Camaro that I only drove once.

"I got my life together, Sha. I told you I'm done now. My homie, Jonny, next in line for the throne. I'm turning everything over to him. In fact, I'm considering moving to Chicago to be close to you and my son," Benz said.

"Well, only time will tell," I answered.

I was hoping what he said was true. With him in the same town, I wouldn't mind letting him keep Junior. However, he would have to prove himself first.

"So, when I move back, can we work on us?" he asked.

"Boy, bye. There is no us. Benz, you lost me years ago. I told you that," I said, growing tired of having the conversation.

"So, you don't think about us?" he asked.

"Sometimes," I confessed. There was a moment of silence.

"Hello?" I yelled into the phone. He was too damn quiet.

"I'm here…just a little taken aback about you saying sometimes."

"Boy, bye," I laughed.

"You know, every time you say 'boy bye' to me, it's because you know I'm telling the truth. Just tell me this… is that still my pussy?" he asked in a serious voice.

"Okay, now you tripping for real, nigga. Kiss my baby for me. I got to get ready to go and hit Nel up," I said.

"Y'all going out tonight?" he teased already knowing the answer.

"Yes, we are," I laughed.

"How are Nel and Angie's asses anyway? I miss my lil' sisters," he said in a playful voice.

"They're good. Nel's ass is getting thicker. You should see your lil' sis. I thought she might've been pregnant, but she's just been working out and eating good."

"Oh yeah? Her ass better not let Mel ass knock her up, especially how that nigga be getting down."

"What? What you mean by that, Benz?" I was all ears now.

"Man, nothing. I'm just saying that nigga ain't trying to better himself. He my boy and all, but damn."

"Yeah, Nel said he's changed a lot since high school… doesn't really treat her like she should be treated," I confessed.

"What? Don't make me come up there and beat that nigga's ass," he said seriously.

"Naw, you good. Besides, she deals with it. He just be in the streets more than he should. You know, how you were?"

"Okay. I'll let that slide because I know you got a smart ass mouth that I used to tame," he laughed. "Oh yeah, my man getting married in two weeks. Money, RJ, Mel, and Cruz supposed to come up here for the bachelor party."

"Aw shit, E finally getting married? That's what up! Tell him congrats," I said.

"Guess I'll holla at Mel about lil' sis then," he told me.

"Aight. Bye, baby daddy," I said before hanging up, knowing his crazy ass likes that shit. After we hung up, I started to think about the time I first met Benz.

He was already a senior when Nel and I were just freshmen in high school. Angie was a junior, so Nel and I hung with her to get to the really cute boys. At first, Angie didn't like for us to follow behind her, but once she saw how mature we were, she let it go. Angie was coming from lunch when Benz asked her to come over to his locker. She knew he wasn't trying to holler because they had a few advanced classes together and became good friends. Although he was sexy, he wasn't Angie's type.

"What up, Brian?" she asked, calling him by his real name.

"Yo', who was them girls you were with after second quarter?" he asked, smiling away.

"Oh, my little sister and our friend," she stated.

"Oh yeah, which one is your sister?" he asked.

"The caramel skin one," she answered.

"Damn, they freshmen then, huh?"

"Yep, but my sister has a boyfriend. You've probably seen him around... Jamel. Everyone calls him Mel, though."

"Yeah, okay. Well, that settles it. I wouldn't want to have them both fighting over me. Hook me up with the friend. She right and thick as fuck, man," Benz said.

"I'll holla at her after school. Be over by your locker, so I can introduce your ass," Angie said, laughing and walking off.

The rest was history. When Benz and I hooked up, we were always together. I became his girl, and Nel and Angie became his lil' sisters. He would do anything for his three girls and had gotten close with Mel since he was Nel's boyfriend. He left to go off to college, and the problems started between him and I. However, somewhere along the way we kept it together and Brian Jr. came about.

My damn phone rang, bringing me back to reality.

"Hello?" I laughed.

"What's so funny?" Nel asked.

"Girl, just got off the phone with your brother's crazy ass."

"Oh yeah? I miss his big head ass... Morris Chestnut, thug looking ass."

I started cracking up because Nel always said he resembled a thuggish looking Morris Chestnut.

"Girl, you getting ready? I'm taking Mel's Porsche tonight since the nigga always in my shit."

Mel helped cop Nel a Ferrari, and that bitch was nice! She had it for about a year, and his ass was always in it.

"Yeah, I'm about to hop in the shower now," I told her.

"Just grab sis and come over after y'all get ready," I said.

"Okay. What you want to sip on?" she asked.

"Um...bring some Cîroc and pineapple juice," I said.

"Alright, bet. See you in a lil' bit, bitch," she said.

"Bye, bitch." I hung up the phone and headed for the shower.

Nel

*A*fter I got off the phone with Sha, I started getting myself ready. I rarely wore makeup but decided on a lil' eye shadow and lipstick from my favorite girl, Keyshia Ka'oir. Mel called before I left the house and told me to have a good time. I was on my way to get Angie, grab our drinks, and head over to Sha's house.

"Y'all bitches look sexy as fuck," Sha said playfully as soon as we walked in.

Angie wore a black dress. I wore a black and beige long-sleeve, mesh, cutout party dress that hugged my body curves just right. I paired it with a black clutch and black heels. Sha wore a red, one-shoulder dress with the back cut out and a cutout in the front. She paired it with a gold clutch and gold red bottoms. We looked sexy as hell. We were flawless beauties with little to no makeup.

We talked a little about the fun we were going to have before we headed to the car. In the car, I played our song, "Bitch, Don't Kill My Vibe" by Kendrick Lamar, to get everybody turned up. Sha started singing along.

"Bitch, don't kill my vibe. Bitch, don't kill my vibe."

"Okay, ladies. Let's drink the last of this drink and head in. Look at that damn line," I said, turning the volume down on the music.

"Man, I'm letting my hair down tonight," Angie confessed.

"Okay, where is my damn phone?" I asked to no one in particular.

"Bitch, right here," Sha laughed, knowing I couldn't go anywhere without my cell phone.

We walked up to the front of the line where the bouncer, Zeek, was standing. The line was just too long to stand in.

"What's up, Nel?" Zeek spoke to me.

Everyone knew Zeek had a thing for me, including Mel. It didn't matter because I was way out of Zeek's league.

"You got our table ready, big boy?" I flirted back with Zeek.

"Yeah, lil' lady, y'all go on in," Zeek smiled, removing the rope between us.

As soon as we got inside, we made our way to the bar. DJ Khaled's "Do You Mind" came blasting through the speakers. The club was packed way beyond capacity, and people were dancing all over. Thirsty females walked around trying to find Illinois' best ballers. The club was filled with men.

There were two floors and an open space in the club reserved for the dance floor. People were hanging by the stairs, throwing money from the top. This was definitely the place to be in the city right now. We got settled at our VIP table at the bar because we knew it would be a while before the bartender made it over to us.

"This shit right here is off the fucking chain," Sha said, grinding in her chair to Beyoncé's "Sorry".

"Let's hit the dance floor," Angie said, as she danced in front of me.

As soon as we hit the dance floor, our song, "Neva End" by Future featuring Kelly Rowland, came on. Sha was grinding up against some sexy dark-skinned nigga.

I started moving my mesmerizing hips, turning down niggas left and right. Suddenly, I felt some arms around my waist, but he wasn't really dancing which made me turn around to see who could be that bold, knowing I belonged to Mel. Every nigga in the streets knew I was off limits. I turned around and was lost for words. The guy in front of me looked similar to my celebrity crush, T.I.

"What's good, lil' mama? Why you stop dancing for a nigga?" the T.I. look-alike smiled. He had the whitest teeth I had ever seen. I was really feeling the third shot I took at the bar because I really started to put on a show for the cutie who I imagined to really be T.I.

"We don't wanna neva end. It's like our life has just begun," I sang, grinding all on the T.I. look-alike.

"What's your name, baby? Don't tell me it's Kelly Rowland with the way you dancing on a nigga?" the T.I. look-alike joked.

"It's Chanel," I yelled over the music.

"That name fits you, lil' mama. You can call me Real, baby," he yelled back.

"Excuse me, you dropped this," some chick said to Real.

"Thanks, sweetie," he said, still holding on to me.

"Aye, this phone yours, lil' mama?" Real asked me.

"Aw shit!" I yelled. "Thanks so much."

"My pleasure," he replied.

The crowd started to really get turned up when they heard Kevin Gates' "Jam" come through the speakers. I looked around for Sha and Angie. I saw Sha a few feet away dancing with the same nigga. Sha eventually walked back over to our VIP with Angie, and I saw them talking to the waitress.

"So, you gon' keep dancing with me?" Real asked.

"I guess, although you're not really dancing," I said, laughing.

"That's cuz I don't dance, lil' mama, but I couldn't let you get away without getting your number," he flirted with a cheesy grin.

"Who said I was going to give it to you? Besides, I have a man, and I can't believe you even that bold enough to step to me. Every nigga in here knows I'm Mel's girl," I yelled over the loud music.

"Well, I know of your man, but he doesn't intimidate me. I actually love competition," he smiled, showing his pearly whites again.

"Ha, that's funny, baby. Mel is his own competition. Intimidation should be the last thing you worry about. Sorry, but I have to go. Nice talking to you."

I started to walk off, but he ran behind me and grabbed me around the waist.

"So, you gon' walk off on a nigga? Every female in here staring at you and wishing they were who I'm sweating." I had to look around. The stares I was getting were most definitely jealous ones. I got stares from being Mel's girl but not how I was getting now. I actually felt somewhat impressed. He was a one in a million dude that knew of Mel and still wasn't intimidated.

"Why are you sweating me then?" I asked.

It was a pause before Real said anything. He couldn't take his eyes off me.

"Because, I want your lil' sexy ass in so many ways. I want to be your man."

I laughed.

"Look, you seem like a nice guy, but let me stop you while you're ahead. I'm not the type of chick that cheats on her man. Dancing with you is even too much, so let that be it."

"I need someone like you on my team. Well, let's start off as friends. I mean, every nigga should become friends with the lady that will become his wife," he added.

That comment had me all fucked up. Here is this sexy T.I. look-alike talking about becoming his wife and my own high school sweetheart hasn't even brought it up. I couldn't help but feel some type of way. I don't know why, but I really wanted to get to know him as a friend, but something was telling me he could be trouble, and that wasn't something I needed right now.

"I really don't need a friend. Sorry, but I got to go," I said.

I walked off, and I honestly felt bad for him. He didn't seem like the type that got rejected a lot, but I really needed to get away from him. I was Mel's girl, and I wasn't about to have him out in the streets looking stupid.

"So, who was that dude all in your shit?" Angie asked once I made it over to them.

"Some nigga named Real that can't take no for an answer. He was sexy as hell, though."

"He resembled your make believe husband, T.I.," Angie teased.

"Girl, my boo, T.I., knows about me, and girl he really does look like him. That's why I had to get the hell away before I did something that I'd regret."

"Bitchhh," Sha said, laughing and dancing her way back up in her seat. "I saw the lil' sexy nigga you was grinding on," she teased.

"Girl, that nigga… but shit, he a G for that shit he pulled, rolling up on me and he knows who Mel is," I said, sipping on my drink.

"Well, it's just a lil' fun. Ain't like you going home with the nigga," Angie mentioned.

"Shit, that nigga acted like he wanted me to," I said but came to a stop when I saw Real coming toward our table. "Girl, this nigga can't take a hint. He's coming over here."

Sha and Angie both turned around and looked in his direction.

"Girl, this nigga crazy," Sha laughed loudly.

We all watched as he made his way to us and spoke.

"What's up, ladies? Y'all looking nice tonight. Y'all having a good time? Y'all need anything else to drink?"

That's all Sha needed to hear.

"Sure, order a few rounds of shots," she said, smiling.

"Okay, I got y'all. If y'all ladies want, you could join our table over there in VIP," Real said, pointing to his crew of niggas.

"Sure, if y'all don't mind?" Sha said, looking at me and Angie.

I was looking like *bitch, why you put me on front knowing this nigga trying to holler*, but I knew Sha was tipsy.

"I guess… if Angie's cool with it," I said, looking at Angie, hoping she would say, naw, let's stay at our own damn table.

I guess Angie was feeling herself too because she grabbed her clutch and drink and stood up. Real led us over to his table, introducing us to his boys right away.

"Yo', Saun, EL, Blue, this here is…" he said, pointing to Sha so she could say her name since he didn't get it.

"I'm Da'Sha," Sha said.

"I'm Angie," Angie said as she looked over at me.

They waited for me to say my name and not be rude.

"This here is my future wife, Chanel," Real said. I guess I was being stubborn and taking too long to respond.

"Ha! You funny!" I laughed.

"Have a seat, ladies," El spoke up.

We all sat down to get comfortable while Real waved over the waitress to get some shots going around. I think he was trying to loosen me up a bit.

"So, y'all live around this area?" Sha asked, breaking the silence.

"Yeah, not too far away… downtown Chicago," El replied, looking like he wanted to eat Sha alive.

"Okay, that's what's up. You look real familiar," Sha said.

"Oh yeah? Well, if I've seen you before, trust me, I would've remembered," El said and stared at her.

We all listened as the DJ mentioned the next song being a request for his dancers out on the floor.

"This my shit," El said when Drake's "Motto" came on.

That nigga got up and started two-stepping. We started cracking up. Even I was starting to have a good time. Angie was getting acquainted with Saun's sexy ass. To be honest, she really wanted to test the waters. She has mentioned a few times that RJ was starting to push her further away, but I always shrugged her off thinking she was just mad at RJ.

"So, lil' mama, you having a good time?" Real asked, looking in my eyes.

"Yeah, it's cool," I said.

"So, can I be your friend?"

"Boy, you just can't understand the word no!"

"Well, you never said no, baby, you just tried to walk off on a nigga. Look, peep game, I watched your sexy ass walk in here and hit the dance floor. Now, you would never catch me on the dance floor, but for you, I made that exception," he said as he licked his lips.

I couldn't do anything but smile. He smelled so good, and I was feeling him whether I liked it or not. I never got close to any other nigga like I was with Real, but then again, I never gave them the time of day. They weren't confident or bold like Real. I could understand why that was his name.

"Here are your drinks, baby," the waitress said, being extra friendly. "So you gon' give me that ride home, right?" she asked Real.

"Yeah, I'll swing back through after you get done here."

This nigga had the nerve to be flirting with the bitch right in my face.

"Okay," she walked off with an extra sway in her step.

I felt a little awkward and surprisingly, a little jealous, and I couldn't understand why.

"Is that your girl?" I asked calmly.

"Naw, just a friend."

"Oh, like you asked me to be?" I asked and Real laughed at me.

"Naw, she gon' stay a friend. I'm trying to be more than that with you, but friends is where we draw the line since you got a man, right?" Real said with his arms now around me.

"Well, I mean...you want to hang with me and my girls? Because that's what my friends do?" I asked.

"I guess...as long as I'm spending time with you," he said, smiling.

I took my shot when Sha handed it over to me. I couldn't comment on Real's last statement because I didn't know what to say. I had a good man at home, or at least I thought so, and here this nigga was feeding me mad game.

"So, can I get your number? I would like to get to know you better," Real asked me.

"Boy, you are crazy," I said not wanting to say yes or no.

"Look, no disrespect, but I'm not going to keep being your boy," he teased.

"It's just an expression!" I laughed.

"Yeah, okay!" he said as he looked around the club.

"Tell me a little about yourself," I said, getting his attention back.

"Well, I'd rather do that over dinner."

I was smiling and blushing. I couldn't say anything. I had been asking Mel for a minute now about taking me out to dinner.

"I don't think that's a good idea."

"Why, because you got a man or because you afraid?" he asked.

"Afraid of what?" I asked, waiting for this response.

"Afraid that I might be the one to steal you away."

"Haha! Yeah, you crazy. What makes you think I'm up for grabs, Real?"

"Well, first off, you still talking to me. Second, you up in this bitch meaning only one thing—your man ain't handling his business at home because right now, me and you would be leaving from a romantic dinner heading home, so I can blow your back out," he said closer to my ear.

I had to admit his theory about me was on point. If Mel was handling his business, I would be doing just that. Real was making my pussy wet, and that wasn't sitting well with me. I needed to turn this conversation around.

"Real, I can't do this," I said, getting up.

My buzz was fading. I took another shot before I asked the

ladies to hit the dance floor with me again. They started playing Kelly Rowland's "Kisses Down Low." We were dancing and niggas started surrounding us trying to get a dance.

I look up at Real and couldn't help but feel something for him. I liked his swag, but I knew I was out of my league with him. I just couldn't take it there with him.

"Damn, my baby moving those hips." I heard El say over the music. "Yo, I'm about to go get my new boo."

I saw Real and El coming our way. I had to admit, Real wouldn't give up, and I liked it. Sha started dancing up on El while I stared into Real's eyes.

"What? You shy now? You gon' dance with me or what?" Real asked.

I grabbed Real and started dancing. I knew them damn shots would sneak up on my ass.

"I like my kisses down low, makes me arch my back," I was singing when Real kissed my neck. I almost lost control of my knees, but he was holding my ass tight and close. I knew this was wrong on so many levels, but damn, it felt good to have someone's undivided attention.

"Stop teasing me, baby. Daddy doesn't like that," he joked. "So, can I call you sometimes? Take my number," he pressured again.

Real handed me his business card. I took it and glanced at it.

"Wow, you're an entrepreneur?" I asked.

"Don't seem so surprised. But yeah, I run about twelve businesses.

Let me guess…you thought I was a drug dealer?"

"Um, I mean…I assumed, but I guess—"

"You guessed right," Real laughed. "I'm smart, though, so I'm legit with it."

I was confused about my feelings. I really needed to get far away from him. I knew nothing about this nigga, but somehow I wanted to keep in touch with him.

"Okay, um, I'll call you—" I began saying, but I locked eyes with Mel's ass, and I wanted to damn near disappear. Real eased his arms around my waist, but Mel couldn't see what he was doing because it was so crowded.

Jamel

"Man, fuck them duck bitches. Candy's ass on her period," I said.

"I'm not about to be sitting in them bitches face, and we can't hit nothing," Money stated.

"That's what I'm saying let's hit the club up. Ain't shit else popping tonight," I said. "Nel's ass got my car. I wanted to stop through the car show tonight."

"Nigga, you always in her shit. Is she supposed to ride with her girls all the time?" Money said as he puffed on the loud they were smoking.

"Naw, my baby good. I'm just saying," I said, looking at RJ. "Man, what the fuck you over there thinking about? Your ass been quiet all night," I asked.

"Shit, man, Angie's ass been tripping, on some disrespectful shit," RJ finally confessed.

"Man, you got to take care of home. She's supporting your ass right now. Of course, she's losing respect," I schooled him.

"Man, shit, that's easy for y'all niggas to say. It ain't easy losing a mother. I'm working on myself," RJ said.

"RJ, I been telling you to get back in the game for a while. I know you said it's a conflict of interest being that Angie is a lawyer. However, that shit can be beneficial too, nigga!" I said, hoping my boy cheered the fuck up. I didn't want him to start getting all emotional about his mom dukes. I didn't know how it felt to lose a mother, so I couldn't tell him how to handle the situation.

"Man, y'all niggas need to come on. We got an hour to party in this bitch!" Money spoke up, getting out the car.

We made our way in, and of course, bitches were being thirsty as fuck. I looked around the club and I locked eyes with Nel. I wished I was strapped because I would've deaded that nigga, Real, in front of everybody and dealt with the consequences later. I knew who Real was. He had the biggest connect in Chi-town right now. I made my way through the crowd.

"Yo, nigga, I'm not even gon' ask why you all in my girl's face because I'm gon' assume you got a death wish or some shit!" I looked at the nigga with fire in my eyes.

"Yo, man, calm that tender shit down. We were just dancing," Real said.

"Nigga, fuck you. I saw how you was all over my shorty. I'm not gon' say the shit again." I grabbed Nel by the arm, pulling her away from him.

"Yo, hit me up, Nel!" Real yelled.

I looked at Nel, and I knew she wished his ass didn't say that shit.

"Yo, you got the nigga digits?" I asked, looking dead at Nel.

This bitch must want to join this nigga in his grave. I thought to myself.

"It's just a business card, baby. Let's go!" Nel said, walking away.

When she noticed I wasn't behind her, she turned around, but it was too late. Real and I were throwing down. Real's crew was making their way over and so was RJ and Money. If anyone knew my nigga, Money, he stayed strapped. He would pay the bouncer three racks to not search him. Nel ran and grabbed me.

"Jamel, please stop. Let's go. He ain't worth it, baby!" she yelled.

RJ grabbed me and Blue grabbed Real. I could tell Blue was the calmer one in their crew because Saun looked like he wanted to go head up with us. That nigga, Real, wasn't a hoe ass nigga and neither was I, so you can only imagine how the fight went.

Money looked at Saun and said, "Look man, dead that shit."

Saun knew that Money was not to be fucked with. He was the partner of Kingpin Benz. I walked off pissed at Nel and more at Real.

Outside, Nel and I were going at it.

Finally having enough, Money said, "Take that shit home! Motherfuckers peeping that shit out."

Nel got in my car and was about to pull off, but I snatched the door open.

"Man, you know I'm not about to let your ass drive home drunk," I said while grabbing the keys out the ignition.

"Who said I was drunk?" she yelled at me.

"That better be the reason as to why you were all over that nigga."

Nel got over to let me drive. I had RJ drive Nel's car with Angie, Sha, and Money. I called RJ and told him to just take the car home with him and I'll just grab it tomorrow. I didn't need for everyone to be in on our mess.

I looked over at my girl. She was golden. I knew that. I knew if I didn't change my ways, I would lose her. I knew I needed to leave the streets and the other bitches alone completely. Otherwise, my relationship would end just like Benz and Sha's.

"Nel, you want to talk?" I finally spoke, breaking the silence in the car.

"Not really, Mel!"

"What? Well, you better say something before I slap the shit out your ass for being all over that nigga!" I said with a little more bass in my voice.

"Nigga, you smoking that shit you sell? You so much as lay a hand on me, I'll kill your ass then call my brother Benz to bury your body!"

I looked at Nel and laughed. I knew just how to piss her lil' ass off. But true enough, I would never put my hands on Nel. Not just because of Benz, but because I could never hurt her physically.

"Man, all I want to know is why, Nel? Why?"

"Why what, Mel?"

"Why were you all over that nigga, Real? You dancing on that nigga like you want to throw my pussy that way!"

"Really, Mel?" was all her lil' ass had to say.

She didn't think I saw all of that shit. She just knew that she had locked eyes with me before I saw her.

"Naw, really. What the fuck was you thinking?" I asked.

"I was just dancing. Damn, Mel," she answered.

"What the fuck you breathing all hard for like you tired of hearing me? Yo' ass the one shaking, laughing, and whispering in that nigga's ear."

"Mel, please. It was a dance, okay?"

"You got something you want to tell me about you and ol' boy? Y'all looked well acquainted with me."

"Lord, he was telling me about his businesses. He's an entrepreneur, and he also has some hands in real estate. He overheard me and Sha talking about the house we were looking at."

"Okay, but where does he come in at? You know I'll drop the cash for that shit with no questions."

"Okay, but we were supposed to be watching what we cash out on. Remember being careful and smart like Benz said?"

I knew Nel had a point so I let the shit go, but I was going to keep tabs on that nigga, Real.

"Okay, baby. If you say that shit wasn't anything, then it wasn't nothing. Give me a kiss, baby," I said, reaching over to kiss her lil' sexy ass.

"Besides, I know can't no nigga replace daddy, right?" I asked, already confident Nel would never leave me.

"You right, daddy," she half smiled.

When we made it home, I made love to Nel like I never have

before just so her ass would know she could never replace daddy. After a hot shower, we cuddled and she fell asleep. My phone started vibrating, but I didn't want to wake her, so I ignored it and passed out shortly after.

Real

I was pissed that nigga, Mel, ran up on me. I didn't want revenge, but my nigga, Saun, couldn't let the shit go. The nigga was too trigger happy if you asked me. I knew what battles to seek out and which ones to leave alone. Everyone knew Money and Mel were Benz's people. Benz made it known not to fuck with his crew. Saun was hot tempered, but I was the thinker in the group. I knew how to settle things.

I couldn't get my mind off Chanel. She was a real woman, and I knew I crossed the line trying to get at her, but I felt Mel didn't deserve a woman like her. I knew if Chanel were mine, I would drop all them hoes I fuck with and treat her like the queen she is. I knew it would be a matter of time before Chanel found out about how Mel was fucking with Candy because a lot of people was talking about it in the streets. I looked at my phone and stored her under Chanel. I would make my move at the right time. Although I wanted to call her, I knew I couldn't. I never had to chase a bitch this hard before, but then again, I never met anyone like Chanel before. All I could do is wait for the right opportunity to present itself then go in slowly. I sat on my boy, El's, step, thinking to myself.

"Man, why you sweating that nigga's bitch? You know that's his girl!" Blue spoke too pissed.

Blue wasn't a scary nigga. He just knew when shit was right and wrong, and this shit would surely start something.

"Man, that nigga don't know what to do with a woman like Chanel. I damn sure didn't see a ring on her finger!" I said.

"And you do, nigga?" El chimed in.

"Man, fuck y'all! I got to swing back by the club and grab Sherry's ass," I said, getting up to leave.

"Oh, so you couldn't get Chanel, so you'll just settle for Sherry's ass?" El joked.

All the men started laughing.

"Man, fuck y'all. She got that super head, nigga," I laughed and walked to my car.

"Yo', Blue, you riding? I'm not coming back through here," I told Blue.

"Yeah, might as well get me some super head too!" Blue said.

Blue and I made our way to the club and parked around the back. As soon as we parked, Sherry was walking up to the car.

"Thanks, Real, for picking me up. I can't wait until my car gets out the shop," she mumbled with her breath smelling like alcohol.

"Yeah," I responded. She has been talking about that car for a year now.

As we pulled up to Sherry's house, she knew the deal. She was about to give us some fye ass head or some lettuce as Stevie J from *Love and Hip Hop* would say. I went with Sherry to her room first. She wasted no time taking my pants off.

"Damn, girl, suck daddy's dick…just like that…yeah."

Sherry had my eyes rolling in the back of my damn head with my toes curled and all.

"Ahh, ahh," I moaned as I shot my seeds down Sherry's throat.

"Hey, Real, you think you can loan me $300? I'm short on my rent this month."

"Man, you asking me for a loan knowing damn well you ain't gon' pay shit back. I told your ass to keep it upfront with me if you need it just ask."

"Okay, can I get $300?" she rephrased.

I pulled out a knot of money and handed her begging ass three crispy one-hundred-dollar bills. I walked out and sent my boy in.

"Aye, man, I hope you got some cash on you. Her ass begging again," I joked at Blue.

It took Sherry's ass no time to make Blue cum. He was walking out within five minutes. I laughed and headed for the door while Blue shook his head at me.

"She got my ass for $250," Blue laughed.

"You $50 richer than me, nigga!" I laughed, walking out the house.

Sherry was a bust down, a sexy ass bust down, but she had the best head game in the city. I met her at the club and brought her back to one of our spots. Not only did she let me hit it, but she let my whole crew hit one night, and we were eight niggas deep. That day, I made a mental note to never fuck her again, but she was good for head, though. I was going to drop Blue off, but we had a meeting with this connect from D.C., so Blue decided to kick it at my crib.

Blue and I were good friends from back in the day. We got in a fist fight and after that had mad respect for each other. He was my brother that was for sure. Now my nigga, El, that nigga was my brother. You had a problem with him, you had one with me.

I took a quick shower, warmed up my plate I got from my mom's that day, and laid across my bed. I wanted nothing more than to have a woman at home, but I didn't want just any woman. Shit, I wanted Chanel. I'd seen Chanel a few times, but she was always with her girls. I was going to step to her until I found out she had a man. Shit, the whole city knew that she was Mel's girl. However, at first, I was a little curious to know why I've never seen them together.

I often went out to eat, whether it was with a chick or by myself. I saw Money a few times with a female he was gaming, even RJ and his girl, who now I know is cool with Chanel. I wonder why I never ran into Mel and Chanel. I turned my TV off and sat in the dark thinking about Chanel lying in my arms. I couldn't believe that I was sweating her like this, but when you've found the one, you just know. I never had to sweat any chick before. Then again, Chanel was a different breed from these other females, and she was one of a kind. I would have to get over my little ass crush for her, or I would end up hurting myself in the long run.

Angie

I was in the shower when RJ walked into the room. He sat on the bed. He used to make me so happy. After his mom died, he kind of put a pause on life. He was slacking at work and got fired because they felt he didn't care about the clients he had. RJ was working for a real estate company that made a lot of money.

When he missed four straight showings for some very expensive houses, they gave his ass the boot. I had his back, though. I did everything I could to try to keep him together, but that was four years ago. I was tired of working overtime to support us both and paying off my $50,000 settlement from being sued from totaling out a BMW because I was texting while driving. No one was hurt, but at the time, my pockets were. We also had a four-bedroom home that he talked me into buying. We actually got it for a good price in a good suburban area, but now I'm stuck paying all the bills.

Now, we can't even have a decent conversation without arguing about what he ain't doing. We haven't made love in over a month. It's been more like a quick fuck every once in awhile.

"You got out the shower fast as hell. I was going to join you," he said.

"Well, I'm done now, so that's not gon' happen!"

I walked past RJ, grabbed my towel, and sat on the sofa in our room. I began to add moisturizer to my body. RJ quickly jumped in the shower and was out within fifteen minutes. He quickly dried off and walked inside my walk-in closet to where I was.

"Hey, baby. I love you, girl!" RJ said, wrapping his arms around me.

"RJ, I'm trying to find an outfit for tomorrow."

"Where are you going? I wanted to spend some time together and maybe go out to dinner and catch a movie afterward…if you'd like?"

"I'm going out to lunch with Nel and Mom tomorrow," I huffed like RJ was irritating the hell out of me.

"Okay, but we can do dinner later that night? My treat. Baby, come on, we haven't spent quality time together nor had sex in a while."

"RJ, you need to save your little money, because I'm not gon' keep supporting your lil' habits. You really need to quit smoking weed and see about finding a job!"

RJ stared at me like he wanted to slap the shit out of me.

"Angie, I'm trying. I got some things set up, and I'm fucking tired of you disrespecting me just because you bring in the income. Don't forget I helped pay your damn tuition when you were in law school, so your ass didn't have to take out any student loans. I paid $30,000 when that bastard took your ass to court so they wouldn't start garnishing your checks and you could make payments on the rest. You totaled his car because of texting, not me. So, before your ass starts talking about what you do now, think about who the fuck got your ungrateful ass there!"

He walked passed me. I wasn't sure if he was leaving the house or just in another room. I didn't hear any keys, so I knew he was still here.

I was upstairs getting my wife beater and boy shorts on. I felt bad. I knew I was wrong but at the same time, I felt that it was time RJ got himself together. I know his mom died years ago, and I didn't know how it felt to lose a mom, but I just wanted more for RJ. He was depending on me way too much. However, I know I was being a straight bitch. I was hitting below the belt. I decided that if our relationship was going to go further, I needed to play my part in it. I haven't really been a great supporter either.

RJ cussing my ass out did put me back in my place. That's why I fell in love with him; he could handle me when those other niggas couldn't. And no, I'm not the one that likes a nigga going upside my head to prove his love for me, but damn, don't let me run all over you, which is exactly what has been happening with RJ and I. I guess because I was footing the bills, he felt like he wasn't wearing the pants anymore.

I grabbed my robe but decided to leave it. I wanted my man to see what he would be losing if he didn't get his shit together. I crept downstairs and saw RJ's head laid back on the sofa with his eyes closed. I thought he might've have been asleep until he took a sip of his drink.

"You still drinking? I know you and the crew already had some drinks," I asked.

"See, there you go jumping to conclusions again. We smoked some loud and was gon' get our drink on in the club, but that shit was cut short with that shit your sister pulled!" RJ said, laughing a little.

"Naw, my sister ain't pulled shit. Your boy was just scared he was gon' lose sis!" I laughed. "But I came down here to talk to you about us,"

I said, looking in his eyes.

"Man, on some real shit, Angie, you hurt me with that shit you said upstairs. I never thought I would see the day you disrespect me and hurt my pride!"

"RJ, please let me talk, baby. Just listen. I'm grateful for all you've done for me and how you helped me get to where I'm at now. You lost someone who meant the world to you, and as your girl, I should've shown more sympathy. I should have been there for you like you've been there for me. I love you, baby, and I am so sorry that I made you feel that way! Please, forgive me. I want to move forward with our relationship, but I need you to get yourself together because it's starting to affect our relationship." I had tears in my eyes now.

"Angie, thanks for saying that, but that doesn't change the fact that I'm still beyond hurt. I love you more than anything. You out of all people knew how close I was with moms."

It was silent for a minute.

"I'm hoping to go into business with Gary since he needs some help running his business. I know it's time I get myself together!" he said. RJ reached over and pulled me onto his lap. "I miss you so much, baby. I need you," he confessed.

I looked into my man's eyes and started slowly kissing him as he started rubbing my legs and kissing my neck.

"I miss you too, baby," I moaned.

RJ stood me up and slid my boy shorts off. He was still on the couch and he kissed my stomach, making his way to my belly then made his way down to my thighs. He told me to lie on the couch and I wasted no time.

He began sucking on my sweet nectar.

"Oh, you taste so good, baby," he said.

"Oh my goodness, RJ. Please just give me the dick…um, baby, I don't want to cum now."

RJ was sucking and licking just right, and I couldn't help but cum all on his tongue. I came long and hard while he was still sucking like his life depended on it. He finally got up and got ready to stick his ten inches into me when I stopped him. "Baby, it's been a while; let me please you too, daddy," I said.

I was stroking him with my hand as my lips touched the tip of his head. I slid my lips up and down, sucking his dick like a popsicle. I started deep throating and increased my bobbing speed.

"Aw shit, baby, damn. Ahh…ahh…ahh…yes…damn, a nigga miss that shit."

"Oh, but that's not it, baby."

I climbed on top of RJ and started riding him reverse cowgirl style.

"Yeah, baby, ride your dick. It's yours," he said, breathing harder.

He flipped me on my stomach and pounded my pussy from the back.

"Yeah, throw that ass back for daddy, baby!"

We went at it for as long as we could until we both cuddled on the couch and fell asleep in each other's arms.

Da'Sha

$\mathcal{I}$ was out of the shower, lying around naked. I did that whenever my son, Junior, wasn't around. I was checking my Facebook when I read my classmate's status about almost being done with school. I couldn't wait either. I checked my messages and had four unread messages. There was one from EL, who I met at the club tonight, and three from Benz. I read the messages from Benz.

Benz: *Hey, baby. I hope you got in ok. Your son shitted every damn where today, but he all good now.*

Benz: *Hey, give me a call when you can…tonight if you want.*

Benz: *Your son wants to say goodnight.*

The next text came through while I was reading his previous messages

Benz: *Baby, just making sure you got in tonight.*

I decided to call him. I had to admit I was missing him, but I would never ever tell his crazy ass that. I felt like Benz chose the streets over me and expected me to wait until he was ready. Shit, life didn't work like that for me.

"Yo', what up?" Benz groaned into the phone.

"You sleep? I can call you tomorrow," I told him.

"Naw, I was just laying down. You good, baby?" he asked.

"Yes, so what up? You texted me and said to call you, so what you want, baby daddy?"

"You always calling me damn baby daddy. I'm still your man whether we're together or not!"

"Oh yeah, but that's not why you said to call you!" I laughed.

"Actually, it is. I miss you and been really thinking about moving to Chicago and working on us again. I never stopped loving you. You're the one who left me."

I really didn't know what to say. He talked about moving to Chicago plenty of times. I didn't want to have this conversation because I always ended up hurt from broken promises.

"Benz, look, we've had this conversation often, but you always manage to fuck it up. Tell me, why I should believe that you gon' do right by me? Besides, you have another child down there that needs you more than Junior right now!"

"First off, quit talking about shit you know nothing about. I got a blood test on that little girl, and she ain't mine. And as far as Junior not needing me, my son will always need his father. I don't even know why you let that shit roll off your tongue!"

"So what happened...the lil' girl is what...four now? So, you just stop playing daddy after she got attached to you?"

"No. I had my reason to think she wasn't mine, so I was distant from the beginning. Only thing I did was support her financially, but when that DNA test came back, and I found out that bitch lied—"

"You put a hit out on her?" I joked.

"Man, don't be talking like that on this phone. You know better than that, girl!" he said.

"Yeah, okay. But to respond to whatever bull you feeding me, I'm happy with my life right now with no drama. Besides, I'm just doing me."

"Doing you as in what? Fucking any and every nigga?" he asked.

Benz knew I wasn't like that. He knew I could party my ass off, but fucking with any nigga wasn't my style.

"So, that's how you gon' play me?" I asked, getting pissed.

"I'm saying…you talking about you doing you. What's that shit supposed to mean?"

"Doing me doesn't necessarily mean me fucking. Maybe I'm just happy with how my life is now!"

"Okay, so you saying you can't be happy with me? Regardless of what we have been through, I always kept you happy, right?"

"Yeah, you did. But there were times you hurt me and chose the street and those bitches over me!"

Tears started forming in my eyes, and I thanked God he couldn't see me.

"Sha, I don't know how many times I can say sorry. I was dumb then, and I let that shit go to my head. I know that I love you and want to make things right between us."

"Make things right? Benz, we're doing what we're supposed to for our son. We don't argue about you seeing him, and you take care of him like you should. That's all that's need to be right."

"Sha, baby, please just give me a chance to be in your life and to give our son a family!"

"Benz, right now I'm focusing on graduating so I can keep my son's life good. You never know with you, so I must stay on my game."

"I know you graduating, baby, and I'll be there yelling your name."

I had to laugh at that.

"I just bet you are."

"Okay, Sha. But maybe when I bring Junior home we can talk face to face because I know you good at hiding your emotions."

"Ha, you think you know me. Tell my son I can't wait to see him and have him call me in the morning."

"Okay, but um…think about what I said, Sha, on some real shit."

"I'm not saying I will, but whatever, Benz. Bye."

"Woman, yeah, I can tell you ain't had no real dick because your ass slick with those lips. I can't wait to bring your ass down a notch."

"Boy, bye! I'm hanging up." I had to laugh as I hung up the phone. My baby daddy was something else.

I grabbed my covers and turned the TV on. I was about to lay my head back when my phone vibrated. I thought it was Benz texting back, but it was El. I read the text and smiled.

El: Hey miss beauty. I hope you had a good time tonight. I wish I could have talked to you longer. I hope that shit that went down ain't ruin my chances with you. Have a good night or morning. Kisses down low is my shit now…lol, gn.

I couldn't do anything but laugh. *Niggas are crazy these days. I thought to myself.* I look at the clock and it was 4:30 am. I figured what the hell and texted him back.

Sha: Hey there! Thanks. I did have a good time tonight and that's what I gave you my number for so we could talk. I just bet that is your song now…lol. Why are you up so late? And no that shit your dude pulled ain't ruin your chances.

I waited for him to respond back.

El: Ha, my nigga ain't pull shit, but that's not what I want to talk about. Glad to know I still got a chance. Baby, this ain't late this early for me. So, can I take you to dinner if you're not busy later today?

I waited a few minutes thinking if I should or not. I went on few dates but none of them had my attention like they should. But I really liked El's swag, so I figured I'd let go and live a little. I texted him back.

Sha: On one condition, we stay away from Chinese food lol.

El: Okay that's cool, but what's wrong with Chinese, lol, you don't like it?

Sha: That's the problem. I like it so much that I eat it every other day. What time would you like to meet?

El: Is 7:30 okay with you? I was thinking Alinea restaurant. Ate there once and love it. Have you been there before?

Sha: No I have not, but I hear great things about it. I would love to go there. See you at 7:30 pm tomorrow. Gn.

El: I hate this texting shit. Can I call you?

I was going to text back 'yeah' but decided to erase it and call him.

"Hey, sexy," El answered the phone. "You just couldn't wait to call me?"

"Ha, you got jokes. I just don't like texting either, but what's up? I did hear good things about that place. I hear it's very expensive too."

"Yeah, my last bill was almost $500, but that's cool. I want to show you something new."

"Boy, please. I've been to some of the best restaurants on this planet," I laughed.

I knew he didn't know I was Benz's baby mama.

"New you say? Well, we will see," he added.

"So, you got a man?" he asked, getting to the point.

"Fine time to ask after we made plans, don't you think? But no, I'm single at the moment."

"Moment, huh? Well you must be waiting for me to make it official?"

"Official? Don't get ahead of yourself now, sweetie," I said.

"Okay, I'll give you a month before you fall in love with a nigga," El said.

"Yeah, okay, I hear you talking!" I said, yawning.

"You sleepy, baby?" El asked.

"A little, but I'm okay."

"You sure? Naw, I'll let you go to sleep, sexy, so you can dream about us tonight."

I laughed and told him to hold on a moment because my other

line was beeping. He told me as long as I return, he'll wait forever. That made me laugh. I looked at the screen before clicking over, and it was Benz. I thought it may be about Junior, so I answered.

"Hello?" I answered the phone.

"Hey, girl, what you laughing at? You must be on the phone with Nel's ass?" Benz asked.

I felt like I had no reason to lie, so I told the truth.

"Naw, Nel probably at home with Mel's ass arguing about the shit that went down at the club. And I don't feel like getting into that so holler at your boy Mel tomorrow!" I said, trying to rush him off the phone.

"Well, who are you talking to, Sha?" Benz asked.

"None of your damn business, Benz…a friend. So what do you want?"

"The fuck, a friend? As in a male friend? At five o'clock in the morning!" Benz asked, sounding like he was getting pissed before I could even answer.

"Benz, that's none of your business. Why are you calling me is what I want to know, and is Junior okay?"

"Naw, fuck that. Who are you talking to? I ain't gon' ask you again. I'll be in my jet, and I'll be there in no more than thirty minutes, so you better tell me something!"

All I could do was breathe hard. I knew he would because his ass was crazy like that.

"Look, yes it's a male, and he's only a friend, Benz, damn!"

I was pissed now because we weren't together, and I felt I didn't have to explain shit to him.

"Tell that nigga night, night then, Sha. Ain't shit to talk about this late but sex, and that's not gon' happen!"

"Boy, who the fuck you think you talking to? We ain't together. I'll call your ass back later!"

I hung up on Benz and clicked back over to El.

"I'm sorry about that, El," I said, "but yeah…I'll see you later. it was good talking with you."

"It's good, ma. I told you I'll wait. I enjoyed talking with you, have sweet dreams, baby."

We hung up and my phone started ringing again. I knew it was Benz, so I thumbed his ass only for him to call four more times before he left me a voice message. I laughed to myself when I heard him say he would find out who this nigga is and there would be hell to pay if he hitting his pussy. I knew his ass had reached a new level of crazy. I dozed off to sleep thinking about El.

Chanel

I was getting dressed for the day. I was meeting my mom and sister later for lunch, but first, I wanted to make Mel some breakfast in bed. When I woke him up, he wasn't surprised. I did stuff like that for him all the time. He went into the bathroom and brushed his teeth. I went back downstairs and sat on the couch to watch the news to see how the weather would be.

I grabbed my phone and the side of it was cracked, which brought back the memory at the club when Real handed it to me. I thought about how bold he was and how if his boy didn't grab the two men, some damage would've been done. I felt like I owed him an apology, but why? I didn't know, but something was telling me I would see him again.

"Thanks for the breakfast, baby," Mel said and kissed me on the cheek, interrupting my thoughts.

"Hey, baby. You still taking me out to dinner later tonight, please Mel?" I begged.

"Yeah, but if we got to handle business tonight with this new connect, then I don't want you to be disappointed, okay, baby?"

I felt like he was lying. My woman's intuition was telling me he was a damn lie, but I was a fool when it came to him.

"Okay, baby," I said.

I was on my way to pick up my mom and Angie so we could do lunch.

"Hey, Mom." I got out the car and hugged my beautiful mom. I was identical to my mom, except my mother was a tad bit lighter than Angie and me.

"Hey, baby, it's good to see you," she said.

We got in the car to head toward Angie's house.

"Chanel, baby, you're almost done with school, and I know you got exams coming soon. How are you doing with your classes?"

"I'm doing good, mom. I'm just happy to be almost done. It has been a stressful four years, but I did it."

"Baby, you and your sister make me so proud. Lord knows I thought raising two teenagers would be the death of me!" Glory joked.

"Oh Mom, we weren't that bad as teenagers," I laughed. "Well, maybe I wasn't," I joked again.

"So, how are you and Jamel doing, baby?" she asked.

Despite how we made up last night, I wasn't completely happy. I wouldn't tell my mom that, but I knew my mom could read past a smile when it came to her girls.

"We're good, mom. He's Jamel," was all I could think to say.

"He's still slanging those damn drugs around town?"

"Mom, he doesn't sell drugs."

I said that to any and everybody. I never talked about my man's hustle, no matter who it was.

"Okay, baby, if you say so. Just be careful. That lifestyle brings a lot of bad and temporary good; trust me, I know."

I wanted to end the conversation with my mom because I knew that my father would come up. Angie's and my father was a drug dealer. When he was building his way up, he was a family man. As soon as he got the money, fame, and power, he started sneaking to different states having affairs, having other children and neglecting his family until my mother up and left his ass. Now, he's in California with who we assume to be his third baby mama. We weren't interested in knowing about our supposed to be brothers and sisters. We felt any kids outside of our mother's home didn't matter.

"Mom, I don't want to talk about this. You know what it would end with."

"Okay, baby. But after graduation, I hope Jamel plans to marry you because I want some grandchildren."

My mom always got excited when she talked about us having babies.

"Lord, here you go. Mom, a baby is a big step, and marriage is a bigger step. You have to want to be with the person for the rest of your life to get married."

I knew I fucked up when I said that.

"Oh, so you don't want to spend your life with Jamel?"

"Mom, that's—" She cut me off.

"Look, Chanel. You don't have to pretend with me. I'm your

mother, I can see behind that mask you be wearing. Baby, if you're not happy and you continue down this path, one of you gon' end up hurt. And if it's you, me and Jamel gon' have a problem!" I couldn't do anything but laugh. Even if my mom was right, I loved Mel more than anything.

We pulled up to Angie's house and my mother stayed in the car while I went to get Angie. I rang the doorbell and waited for my sister to answer.

"Hey, what's up, Nel?" RJ said, opening up the door.

"Hey, tell me she ready?" I laughed.

"Yeah, she's ready."

RJ and I both watched as Angie came down wearing a nice sundress. It was pretty warm to be May. Angie gave RJ a kiss goodbye, and she headed to the car with me. Angie opened the passenger side door and hugged our mom.

"Hey, my baby, it's good to see you," Glory said.

My mother was beyond happy. She loved being with us. She loved to watch us laugh, talk about our lives, and she also loved how nervous she made us when she would read right through us.

"It's good to see you, mom," Angie said, getting in the back seat.

"So, ladies, where should we head? We can grab a bite to eat at the mall, so we can shop, eat, and get our nails and feet done," Glory suggested.

"That's cool," Angie and I said in unison.

"You girls still answer me at the same time. That used to drive me crazy," she said, cracking up.

We walked through the mall, shopping and buying as much as our arms could carry. We grabbed a bite to eat and decided on just our feet for today because Angie had to meet with a client for a hot second to see what this big case would be on Monday.

"So ladies, why don't we talk about relationships? I know you two very well and if you two keep lying, I'm gon' break my belt out for old times' sake," Glory laughed.

"Let's start with you, Angie. I see you wearing that sundress, baby. So, did RJ find a new job, because honey, you're glowing?"

"Mom, yes. There have been some changes, and he's thinking about going into business with his colleague," Angie laughed.

"Oh, that's great, baby."

My mom laughed because I was looking like I was on the verge of a panic attack.

"Girl, settle down. If you two would be honest, I wouldn't have to bust you two out all the time," she said, turning the buttons on her massage chair up and looking at me at the same time.

"Mom, you're crazy!"

"Naw, you funny. Y'all think just because you smile that life won't reveal its true colors. Chanel, you're not happy because Jamel has changed. He's spending more time in the streets, letting these women fill his head up thinking he's the man. He's putting you second, baby."

I was shocked. My mother hit it right on the nose with that one.

"Mom, I don't know about the women part, but yes, most of what you're saying is right."

"Baby, I know you love him, but sometimes you have to let a man know that he's replaceable."

"You see, girls, men think that when they got a good woman and they've been together for so long, that she needs and somewhat depends on him, especially if he's fucking up in the relationship and gets away with it all the time. He thinks he's got you right where he needs you."

"Okay, look at me and RJ's situation. I've been carrying him for so long that I've started to lose respect for him. He's running the streets and living a carefree life while I'm busting my ass to make sure we're continuing to live good!"

"Yes, baby, you're right, RJ is messing up. But you should have pushed him harder but at the same time, been by his side. I'm still here, baby, your mother is still here. His mother is gone. I knew her very well, and I also know that they were beyond close. At that time, he needed you most, but if he's finally getting it together then, baby, don't cry over spilled milk!"

"You're right, Mom, you're right," Angie said.

I sat there thinking. I wished that Mel and I could find some common ground, but Mel's mentality was deep in the streets, and he expected me to go along.

"Mom, how do I get Mel to spend more time with me? I thought I was doing everything that a woman should for her man. Sometimes, he comes homes late into the next morning, and he feels like throwing money in my face will make everything better. I can take care of myself, but he feels like I need him in order to do better."

I looked to my mother for answers because I felt fucking clueless about what I was doing wrong.

"Baby, men like Jamel get themselves caught up. Look at Benz. He was with Da'Sha, and what man would want to lose her. He felt like no one else could take his place; he felt he could get away with hurting her because she allowed him to. You girls are always so quick to shop when your man does something wrong. He throws a few dollars in your face and everything's okay.

Baby, you have to take control. Look at all the signs and listen to your woman's intuition; it'll never steer you wrong. And as far as getting him to spend more time with you, baby, sometimes you got to play with fire. But be careful because you can get burnt."

"Okay, I have no clue to what you're saying," I said with pleading eyes.

"Baby, you ever hear the saying what one man won't do another one will?"

"Yes, but I'm not trying to cheat. What would that solve, Mom?"

I was getting a little bothered that my mother would even consider that an option.

"Chanel, no one is telling you to cheat, but that's the problem. Jamel knows you're not going anywhere. Shit, he took your little virginity and when a man feels like he's not capable of being replaced, there is no limit to what they'll try. Open your eyes, baby. Don't be blinded by love. Lord knows I was many years ago."

I sat back and let the massage chair relax my mind. I knew what my mom was saying, but I couldn't help but wonder is that how Mel really felt. We chatted a little more in the car on the way home as I dropped them off. I thought to myself long and hard about what we discussed and knew something had to change.

Da'Sha

I was thinking about my date with El in a few hours. I had to admit that I was a little nervous. I've been on many dates after the break-up with Benz but it was more to occupy my time. I really wanted to get to know El and that scared me a little. I haven't heard from my girls all day, so I called Nel. I was about to hang up until Nel answered.

"What's good, boo?" Nel said.

"Hey how was lunch with mom? I know that was a lunch date I'll regret missing?" I joked.

"Girl, our mother is crazy you been around my family too long to know just what I'm talking about."

"Girl, I already know," I laughed.

"So, what you got planned for today?" Nel asked.

"Girl, you won't believe me it if told you," I said kind of nervous to tell my best friend about my date tonight.

"Well, try me," Nel responded.

"Girl, you remember the dude that was with Real from the club… the one I was dancing with? Well, we exchange numbers last night and he asks to take me out for dinner." I said sounding excited.

"OMG! Bitch, are you serious? Where y'all going? What you

gon' wear? I want all the details later tonight and I mean all." Nel was speaking so fast, I couldn't do anything but laugh at her.

"Yes, but peep game, we were talking last night and your crazy ass brother called. When I clicked over, I was laughing, and he assumed I was talking to you."

"Sha, I know you did not tell that crazy ass man you were on the phone with a nigga?"

"Girl, you know I've never lied to that man and besides, we're not together. It's time I move on with my life and remove this rope Benz thinks he has around me. Benz's ass snapped when I told him I was on the phone with a friend. He automatically assumed it was a nigga. Then, he asked what else we had to talk about at five in the morning. He said he was going to fly here last night. He on some bullshit. He better go feed that shit to them other bitches," I said.

"Girl, my brother is crazy. I don't know what's wrong with these niggas. Anyway, Mel and I are supposed to go out for dinner too, but you know how that can change in a blink of an eye," Nel said.

"Yeah, y'all should. Ain't shit else to do. Benz ain't said nothing about them meeting the new connect over there, so I don't know what else they got to do that's important. Oh and bitch, I forgot to tell your ass that Benz passed on the throne. Of course, I know he got to take care of loose ends, but he talking about moving here to be closer to Junior," I said.

"Sha, shut the fuck up! No, he's not! OMG! That would be great. I miss that big head Morris Chestnut wanna-be," she laughed and joked.

"It would be good for Junior but as for me, a pain in my ass. He already talking about working on us. Nel, to be honest, I want nothing more to give my baby a family, but Benz fucked up. That baby that was supposed to be his isn't," I said, shaking my head.

"Wait the same baby that cost him all that damn money? That shit is crazy. I got your back whatever you decide, but I'll let you go. I'm about to call and see what excuse this nigga going to have to not take me out, but don't forget to call me and tell me about the date. Oh, which one of Real's boys you going out with?" she asked.

"El's fine ass," I said now excited about the date.

"Oh, okay. I forgot how he looked, but I'm sure he is fine because Real's ass sure is," Nel smiled.

"Uh huh, I knew your ass was feeling that nigga by the way you was dancing with that him. I'm surprised Mel didn't beat your ass when he caught y'all dancing and shit." I laughed.

"Hell naw! He ain't crazy, but I think he was just scared that I actually was talking to the nigga. You know they all know each other, but Mel thinks he can't be replaced."

"They all do," I said before we hung up.

I decided to call Benz to see how my baby was doing.

"Yo', what up, girl?" Benz spoke into the phone. I was happy he was off that bullshit from last night.

"Hey, where is my baby at?" I asked.

"He right here eating some nuggets and fries."

"Okay, put him on the phone," I said not really wanting to talk to Benz.

"Hold on!" Benz said.

"Hey, Mommy, I miss you," Junior spoke with the sweetest voice.

"Hey, baby, mama misses you more, and I love you so much."

"Love you too, Mommy."

"Tell your mama I love her too, lil' man." I heard Benz say.

"Tell your daddy get out of our conversation, baby."

"Daddy, mommy said get out!"

"What she mean get out?" Benz laughed as he got back on the phone.

"I told him out of our conversation," I laughed.

"So, what you doing today? I'm bringing your son home this week because you got too much time on your hands if you talking to niggas late night and shit. If you wanted phone sex, you should've called daddy," Benz teased.

"Look, I called to talk to my son."

"Your son outside playing now, so talk to your man."

I was quiet for a second.

"Oh, so I guess you mad because I said that?" Benz teased me again. "Look, I'll be there the day after the wedding to bring your baby back, so you don't have to make that drive to come get him, but also we got to sit down and talk about some things. My mama said she called you this morning, and your phone was off," Benz stated.

"Oh yeah, it went dead last night, I'll call her later," I said not wanting to respond to the other comment.

"When I get there, we gon' have a talk, so don't be trying to hide from a nigga."

"Boy please, ain't nobody hiding from you, but I'll call y'all later. Kiss my baby for me, please."

"I'll kiss him only if you kiss me when I see you," Benz laughed.

"Benz, stop it."

"What? You don't miss daddy? Damn, that hurts knowing you don't care about your baby daddy."

"Boy, bye," I said.

"Yeah, I'm gon' find out about this nigga that got your ass acting brand new and shit," he said.

I hung up on his crazy ass. I hated when he did that shit, I had to admit I still cared and was somewhat in love with Benz, but I wasn't gon' play the fool for his ass again. I looked at my vibrating phone and he was calling back.

"Why do you take pleasure in torturing me, Benz?" I said as he laughed.

"Sha, ain't nobody torturing you. You just can't keep it real and tell a nigga how you feel, but what I tell your ass about hanging up on me? One day you gon' hang up and never hear from me again," Benz joked.

"Why do you talk like that? If you would stop with those damn comments, I wouldn't have to hang up"

"Girl you know you want this dick—"

I started to hear him say, but I pulled the phone from my ear to see who was calling on my other line.

"Okay, Benz. I'll call you later. I got to go."

I waited until he hung up this time.

"Hello!" I said extra sexy, answering the next call.

"Damn, you sound so sexy. Good afternoon, beautiful. I was just making sure you're not gon' stand me up for dinner in a few hours," El said.

"No, I was just about to take a nice bath and get myself ready, so I'll be there."

"Okay, beautiful. See you in a few," he said.

Those few hours flew by, and I was parked next to the restaurant that I was meeting El at. I text and called El but got no answer. I thought maybe something came up, or maybe he was already inside. Either way, I was going in because I had a nice red dress on and didn't prepare myself to sit at home. I walked in and was amazed at the setting it was beautiful, not that I wasn't used to nice places, but I still was impressed. I walked up to the hostess.

"Hello. Welcome to Alinea Restaurant. What reservation is your name under?"

Shit, I had no clue. I didn't know what name he put the reservations under. I just knew him as El.

"Um…I'm not sure. I'm meeting a friend here, and he didn't tell me what name he made our reservations under."

I felt somewhat stupid. Like, who meets for dinner and doesn't know what name the reservation is under?

"Okay, are you Da'Sha?" the hostess asked.

"Yes, I am." I was happy to know that he did make a reservation and maybe was running late.

"Right this way, Ms. Da'Sha," the hostess said.

I followed the lady to another quiet room with only four tables in it. I noticed El right away, and he was better looking in the light. Once El noticed me, he walked over to me.

"Good evening, beautiful. You looked wonderful. Last night, that dark club didn't do you any justice because you're gorgeous," he commented.

"Thanks. You're very handsome yourself," I said, taking a seat while El pulled my chair out for me.

We ordered our food and both decided on steak and salad.

"So, El, what's your real name?" I asked curiously.

He looked at me and said.

"My government name is Elvin Winston."

"Oh, that's a strong name. I like," I teased.

"Yeah, you better because Mrs. Winston will be you someday," he said, smiling.

I laughed at his confidence. I had to admit it was turning me on.

"You sure do have a beautiful smile." He told me.

"Thank you. So do you."

"Yeah, I plan to make you smile a lot," he said, looking into my eyes.

"Plan? We've been here twenty minutes, and you planning another date?" I said, hoping he was because I was feeling the hell out of him.

"Oh yes, sweetness, I have so much more planned for us," he said as he licked his lips

Now I knew I had to hurry up and get home. My panties were getting wet. He knew what and when to say the right things. Plus, his licking his lips had me turned on. I just hoped he wasn't all talk. Our food came within minutes, and we both ate with little conversation. I guess we were wondering how we felt about each other.

"Da'Sha, I really like you. You're beautiful, smart, and seem to have a good head on your shoulders. We chatted on the phone for hours, but I want to know more about you. Tell me about yourself," he said.

I was in awe. Other dudes that I tried to date wanted to basically know where my G-spot was.

"Well, you know my name Da'Sha and everyone calls me Sha, I'm currently in school. I'm almost done and will be graduating soon. I have a three-year-old son, and I'm twenty-five. You've met my best friends, Chanel and Angie last night, but we're like sisters. We do almost everything together. My mom and dad died in a car accident when I was ten, so I stayed with my grandfather. He basically raised me until I was a teenager then he turned me loose to Ms. Glory," I joked and took a sip of my wine.

"Wow, sorry to hear about your parents. I'mma call you Sha-Sha because I'm not everyone else, and I think your grandfather did a wonderful job with you. Are you and your son's father on good terms and is he the type that trip over his baby mama having a man? Also, if you don't mind me asking, who is Ms. Glory? She must've been something else if your grandfather turned you loose to her."

"Oh no, it's okay. Ms. Glory is Angie and Chanel's mom. She helped raised me. I never met my grandmother; she died before I was born. So, my grandfather was next in line to take care of me."

"Oh, okay. Is Chanel the one my boy was sweating last night?" he laughed.

"Yes, that's her. So, he does like my girl?" I asked.

"Like, I think that nigga in love," he teased.

"Yeah, we have that effect on men," I laughed.

"I believe it," he said, looking into my eyes making me turn away.

"Don't turn away from me, baby. It's the only way I can see the truth in your eyes."

That statement fucked me up. I felt like he could be the one for me. Only time could tell, but I couldn't jump into this without knowing him as well.

"So, tell me more about your relationship with your son's father, and I want to know about your son."

I really didn't like talking about Benz to another nigga, but this one seemed special.

"Well, Brian, my son's father, and I are not together. We are cool, and we get along because we have to for my son, but sometimes he is overprotective of me and my son," I confessed.

"That's natural for a father to want to look out for his son and if that's mean protecting his son's mother, then I can see where he coming from," El smiled.

"Do you have any kids? I asked, eating the last of my steak and red potatoes.

"No, I don't. The last girl I was with had an abortion. That's the closest I've been to having a child."

"Do you want any kids?" I asked.

"Yes, with the right one. I don't want the mother of my child raising our child alone and my child not having a family."

"Yeah, I feel that," I smiled. "So, um…how do you feel about being around a child from a previous relationship?" I asked.

I looked down at my plate because I hoped it wouldn't be a problem because my son comes before anyone.

"Well, if you're asking me if we got serious would I be there and accept your son, the answer is yes. I would be happy to be around him. I'm sure he's a great kid if he's anything like his mommy. Now, I'm not saying I would try to take the role of his father since it seems like Brian is a good father, but I would be there for him," El said.

He was most definitely someone I needed in my life.

"Wow, that's great," I said.

"So, we're almost done here. Do you want to go somewhere and talk, or do you have to get home to get your son?" El asked.

"No, he's out of town with his dad for a few weeks," I said, reaching for the check like it was a habit.

"Yo', what you doing?" he laughed.

"Oh, I was gon' pay for dinner. I'm just used to—"

"Look, I don't know who you've previously dated, but I got this, baby. I asked you to dinner. Now, when you ask me on a date, I'll still pay! Because that's what a man does," he said, cutting me off.

"Well, okay!" I laughed.

"So, you want to walk in the park? It's really nice out," I asked, hoping to spend more time with El.

"Sure, that'll be nice we can hold hands and kiss," he joked.

We waited for the waitress to return with his card so we could leave.

"It really is a beautiful night. I love Chicago at night," I said, looking at the bright lights coming from all over the area.

"Yeah, I love it here too. I'm just looking for someone to share my life with…someone who isn't about games and drama," he said, looking into my eyes.

"Well, I'm not about games, and I'm also looking for someone special," I said.

"You are? Well damn, I thought I was special," El teased.

"I think you're special, but I want to take it slow," I said, looking up at him.

"Well, I'll take it as slow as you would like, but I also like to live in the moment. Every moment should be precious."

I was just staring at him like where did he come from and why did he have to come into my life when things were difficult.

"You know who you favor? I've wanted to ask you that all night!" I laughed.

"Who, and you better not say Michael Ealy!" he said.

I busted out laughing.

"Well, I won't say it, but you do. He's handsome, though…all sexy and shit."

"Yeah, but I want to be known as El, not some celebrity look-alike. That nigga look like me I'm sexier than him anyway." He said eyeing me like he was daring me to say different.

"Yes, baby you are sexier," I said, standing on my tippy toes about to kiss him.

I didn't know what came over me, but it just felt right. We shared a passionate kiss for what seemed like an hour.

"Damn, Sha-Sha, you gon' start something in this park!" he said, walking hand in hand with me over to some benches in the park.

"I usually don't do stuff like this, but with you, I feel like I can be myself," I confessed.

"That's all I ask, baby. Be honest with your feelings."

"So, how old are you?" I asked.

"I'm twenty-seven. Yeah, I need to find my queen a nigga getting old, but somehow I think I found her. I'm just waiting on time, that's all," El said.

"Well, we can only wait," I said.

We talked a little longer in the park before we got into our cars to leave, but not before El stole another kiss from me and promised to plan another date soon. I was so wet driving back home. Damn, I wanted to fuck that nigga in the park. Lord, that's what happens when you haven't had sex in awhile.

Jamel

"*Y*es! Damn, girl that shit felt so good. You got that good shit, baby," I told Candy.

"Yeah, it would've been better if you would have turned your phone off. You got your girl calling every minute." Candy rolled her eyes.

"Look, we just fuck buddies. Don't mention my girl ever again. Don't worry about what she doing, and don't go running your damn mouth to them bitches in the street about what we got going on!" I said.

"Man, ain't shit gon' get back to your girl, nigga. Damn, you wasn't worried about that ten minutes ago!" Candy laughed.

"Yeah, whatever. I'll hit you up. I'm out."

As soon as I got into my car, I called Nel up. I knew she was going to be pissed, I told that girl I would take her out to dinner, but I couldn't pass up on Candy. She been throwing that pussy at me all weekend. Shit, I'm a nigga. I'm not turning down good pussy.

"Hey, Nel. I'm on my way home. Answer your phone, baby. Some shit popped off with Money and them. Call me," I lied

I left a message because Nel didn't answer. I tried four more times but still did not get an answer. I increased the speed on Nel's car. Yeah,

I was cheating in her shit. I ain't shit.

When I pulled up, my car was in the driveway, so I knew she was home.

"Hey, baby, I've been calling you. What's up?" I yelled as soon as I got in the house.

When I got to the living room I couldn't believe my eyes.

"Nel, what's wrong? Why you crying baby? What happened, Nel? Tell me something!" I said, trying to console her.

"Mel, where were you?"

Was all she said. She never even looked up at me.

"And before you lie, I talked to Angie. She and RJ are out on a date, and Money was with some chick, so please come with something that isn't a lie," she said.

I was shocked I didn't think she would call around looking for me. She never did before. I couldn't even call Money to cover for me because Money didn't agree with me cheating on Nel anyway.

"Nel, you know I was meeting this connect. Money didn't want to miss out on the bitch he was fucking, so I went alone," I lied again.

"Oh yeah? What connect because Benz ain't set shit up, and Money damn sure didn't say anything about you meeting no connect because he thought you were at home."

I dropped my head. I could either keep telling a lie or risk telling the truth.

"Mel, where were you?" she yelled.

"Man, I told you. I didn't let Money know about the connect

because Benz told me not to."

"Oh, so if I call Benz, he'll verify your story, right?" Nel said.

"Yeah, but it's late. He probably laying Junior down by now," I said.

"Nope, fuck that! Call him! Matter of fact, I will!" Nel yelled.

She grabbed my phone and called Benz. She knew Benz wouldn't lie and the truth would come out.

"Hello? Hey, brother, I'm sorry it's so late, but it seems as if you have some information that would probably save your boy's life!" Nel spoke into the phone.

I grabbed the phone from her.

"Look, Benz, I'm sorry but your sis tripping. I was supposed to take her out to dinner and shit, but I was meeting that connect you told me about, and I lost track of time. Man, please tell her what's up."

I knew Benz was pissed, but he didn't want to see his sister hurt. He wasn't game on lying, so he didn't. Benz told me to put my phone on speaker.

"Yo', y'all both grown. Don't bring other people into your problems. Nel, if you believe what he is saying, then let the shit go. If not, you deal with that shit like you should," Benz stated.

That's all we heard before the line ended.

"See, I told you," I said.

"Mel, shut your lying ass up. He didn't confirm shit. What he did is not get caught in your lie! So, you sleep on the couch, and I'll be in my bed!" Nel stormed off with tears in her eyes.

"Man, I told your ass where I was. You acting stupid now, talking about sleeping on the couch. I'm getting in my damn bed with my damn girl," I said, trying to hug her from behind.

"Let me go, Mel!"

She tried to push me away, but I was just too strong. She stopped fighting me in gave in. Shit was sweet.

Chanel

I slid from under Mel's gripped and walked around the bed to his side. I grabbed his cell phone and shut the door behind me. His ass didn't even have a password on his phone. He probably knew I would never search his phone. There were a few numbers with no name under them, but I decided to check Mel's text messages. All the messages were erased but three that were sent out. The first one said *I'll be there in ten minutes.* The second message was asking what door to come in. Now, I knew off back that his crew never talked business through texts. I looked at the number he texted and compared it with the number called out. Sure enough, it was a match. I decided to text the number to see what I could find.

Mel: *Hey, I had a good time tonight. Thanks for that.*

I waited for a response. Not even a minute went by before a response came through.

Unknown: *You're welcome. Your girl must've put you out for not answering her calls…Hahaha! I can't wait to taste your nut again. Your pipe game crazy. Gn daddy.*

I was shocked, hurt, scared, and light headed. I knew it all along but my heart wouldn't accept what my mind was trying to tell me. I sat in the living room all night into the morning crying, trying to get a grasp on why would he do this to me. It was 7:32 am when I heard the bedroom door open.

"Nel, baby, why you up so early? You know you still on vacation from work. Baby, come back to bed. I want to make love and make-up from last night," Mel said, walking over to me.

When he got closer to me, I slapped spit out of his mouth.

"I'll be out of here tomorrow. You can have the house. I don't want any memories trying to get over your stupid, sorry ass. I don't have anything to say to you!" I cried.

I got up and threw his cell phone to him. When he looked at the text, he looked at me like *damn, she caught my ass.* He didn't even say anything. I headed to the bedroom to pack my shit. Once I finished, I sat down on the bed and thought about my next move, which would be getting an apartment or condo. It was Monday, so I hurried up and showered and got dressed. I put on some skinny, Levi jeans with a blue and brown blouse. I packed my trunk with as much stuff as I could and walked past Mel's sorry ass.

"Mel?" I called out.

He just stared at me with tears forming in his eyes.

"No, Mel. Please stop. Baby, don't cry. Your ass wasn't crying when you was fucking around on me, was you?"

"Nel, I'm sorry, baby. I'm so sorry. Please don't leave me, baby. Please, I need you," he said, walking toward me.

"Oh, you need me? I needed you for two fucking years to just notice how I changed my hair, or how I worked my ass off in the gym so you could be mesmerized by my ass. I cooked. I cleaned. I helped you get on your feet until you got on top. I was there when you lost your scholarship and started this dope boy shit. All I asked in return was a damn dinner date. Really, Mel? You go out there and fuck the next bitch? You know what? I'm done talking. You jeopardized our relationship since high school to fuck some bitch! You better hope you didn't give me any diseases because I'll cut your dick off and stick it up your ass!" I yelled.

"Nel, I always used condoms, baby."

"You got to be fucking kidding me. You know what? Let's not do this." I grabbed his pants to get my keys to my car off his key ring. I looked at him and said.

"I love you probably always will, but you just lost the best thing that could ever happen to you."

I walked out of the house sat in my car and cried for a good hour before I pulled off.

I rode with the music blasting because I didn't want to think about the situation or hear my cell phone ring nonstop. I knew Mel must've told Money and RJ what happened because everyone was calling.

Sha called the most, but I had important stuff to do like get me condo because I was due back to work next week. I pulled into the office where I was going to buy the condo. I was in there two hours, and it was worth it. By it being toward the end of the month, the office manager agreed to let me move in two days later. I was happy but not with the circumstances. I went straight over to Sha's house. Sha was walking out the house when I pulled up.

86

"OMG! I was about to come look for you. Are you okay, Nel?" Sha asked, hugging me.

"I really don't know, Sha. I really don't know."

"It's gon' be okay. You can stay here. Mel told RJ you packed your stuff." Sha was talking a mile a minute.

"Sha, it's okay, I just got a condo. I move on Wednesday," I said.

"What? So, you're not going to try and work it out? I mean, that bitch probably texted his phone just to start some shit. You know how bitches are these days, Nel."

"What? No, baby, I don't know what Mel told y'all, but let's go inside. You and me both gon' need a drink when I tell you this shit," I said.

An hour went by, and I had told Sha everything. I cried through the whole conversation.

"Oh, hell no! I'm telling Benz right now!" Sha said, walking over to her cell phone. Benz should've just busted his ass out last night instead of letting you find out like this!" Sha said.

"Girl it's cool, but I'm so done with it. It hurts like hell, though, like somebody stole my soul, but I'll take it a day at a time. You know I can't take him back, Sha? I can't and I won't," I expressed, holding in my tears.

"Yeah, we always had a no bullshit policy. You guys have history. Shit, still to this day, I still love Benz," Sha said.

"Yeah, but you two have a child together. You have to talk to and see him all the time."

"As for me, Mel and I don't have anything tying us together, and thank God," I said.

"I'm here for you, sis. No matter what," she said while hugging me.

"I know and thanks. I love you for that."

The doorbell rang, and we looked at each other.

"It's your house," I said while laughing.

Sha walked to the door, and it was Angie. Sha filled our glasses with wine while I repeated the story to my Angie.

Angie was ready to kick Mel's ass. If they all knew me, they knew I was done with Mel.

"It's just sad that we all hang together. It's gon' be really awkward now," Angie said.

"Yes, it is." Sha agreed

"Sha, tell us about El," Angie said.

"Girl, I almost forgot," Sha said, changing the subject.

Sha told us how everything went down from her thinking he didn't show at the restaurant to them kissing in the park.

"OMG! Sha, that's what's up. I'm so happy for you," I said while sipping my wine.

"So, he's taking me to lunch. You guys want to join? I could use extra interrogation for his ass," Sha said.

"I don't know, Sha. He probably wouldn't want us there," Angie said, and I agreed.

"Well, let me text him and find out."

She texted him, and we waited for a response.

"OMG, he said he'll like that. I hope he doesn't expect a foursome," Sha said, causing Angie and me to laugh.

"Well, let me get ready. Do you need to freshen up, Nel?" Sha Asked.

"Naw, I'm good. I might need to wash my face with cold water since I've been crying all day," I said while walking to Sha's bathroom.

We all left together to meet Sha's date.

Once we got there, Sha noticed El's car as soon as we pulled up. We made our way inside the best sandwich shop in town. El waved us over, and we all sat down and got acquainted.

"So ladies, how did I get the pleasure of having three beautiful women to share this beautiful day with?" We all blushed.

"Well, no pleasure from us, maybe just Sha!" Angie teased.

"Wow, y'all said y'all wasn't going to embarrass me," Sha laughed.

"No need to be embarrass. They know you'll be mine soon," El said with lots of confidence.

We all gave El the third degree and boy, was he ready for us.

"Okay, El, last question….do you have any children?" Angie asked.

"No. I mean, I just met the woman of my dreams. I don't want to share her yet," he joked.

Sha and Angie started laughing. I was very quiet, which was

unusual.

"So, Chanel, what troubles you?" El asked.

"Huh, why you say that?" I asked, looking at my cell phone.

"I can read your eyes, and I see that your mind in somewhere else. Whatever it is, you're too beautiful to have such expression on your face. Life is too short. Live, love, and laugh while you can."

El was really good with words which is another reason why Sha liked him so much.

"You're so right, and I'm sorry you guys," I said with tears coming down my face.

"Nel, it's going to get better. El, maybe we should cancel for today. My girl is going through some things right now," Sha said while hugging me.

"No, No, it's okay. Really. It's just those words really got to me. I'm okay, and I'm so sorry, El. I'm not really this messed up all the time."

"It's cool everyone needs to cry every now and then, it helps cleanse your soul. If you don't mind, may I ask what has you so bothered?" El asked.

I looked at Sha, asking if it was okay to trouble him since this was her date. When Sha gave me a smile, I explained everything.

"So, that's it," I said, feeling some relief that I talked to someone outside of my crew.

"Well, I can't explain his actions, but I know he's a man. From what you're telling me, he knows he could get away with what he did, and he knew that you weren't going anywhere. A man knows how to treats his woman. He knows when she isn't happy. My guess is he didn't care as long as he made you happy when it was convenient for him. In his mind, he knew he couldn't be replaced," El said, finishing the last of his food.

"So, he thinks because I dealt with his bullshit this long, so that he could get over on me?" I wanted to know.

"Well, it seems that way. Sometimes, men don't know what they have at home until it's gone, and by that time, she's already moved on to a real nigga," he said.

I nodded my head. I wondered if he meant to throw Real's name in there or if I was thinking too much into it. It was quiet for a brief moment, and El spoke again.

"So Sha, I was wondering if would you like to come to this barbecue I'm having for my boy's birthday on Friday, and you ladies are more than welcome to come," El said, looking at Angie and me.

"So how is Saun?" Angie asked.

"He's cool. He'll be there too. He was talking about you the other day. He said you were cool people."

"Oh, did he? Well, I do have a boyfriend, but he's cool too. How is Real?" Angie said, trying not to look at me.

"Oh, he's good too. That's whose birthday it is. Nel, I know you just got out of a relationship, but quiet as kept, my man digging the hell out of you. What spell did you put on him last weekend?" El joked.

"I didn't do anything to that man. He is something else, though. He can't take no for an answer I know that, but he's sweet," I blushed.

"Are you blushing?" Sha asked.

"Come on you, guys, leave her alone. Besides, my crew has that effect on women, so if you girls decide to come to the barbecue, beware," El warned.

We finished up, and Angie and I walked ahead to give Sha some privacy. We got into the car and watched as El kissed Sha.

"OMG! He is fine, I swear he looks like Michael Ealy from *Think like a Man*," I laughed.

"Girl, I was thinking the same thing," Angie laughed.

Sha got in the car, and we all busted out laughing.

"Sha, he is so sweet. I love my brother, but you better jump on that," I laughed.

"Nel, I know, but it's hard trusting people," Sha admitted.

"Yeah, I can understand that, but he really seems like good people...not the average thugs we're used to," I said.

"Yeah, that's what scares me. It means he's good at hiding his true colors," Sha confessed.

"Yeah, but just see where it goes...you never know," I said.

"You right. I'm gon' give him a chance, and bitch, why when he said something about being in the arms of a *real* nigga you started smiling? Let me find out you thought he was talking about Real on the low. Shit, y'all bitches coming to the barbecue with me. I'll be damned if I go by myself," Sha laughed.

"If he's anything like El, then watch the fuck out because I got claims on that one until I'm ready to start back dating again. I swear it might be forever."

"Nel, if he's anything like El, then this Friday you gon' be a married woman," Angie said and we all laughed.

We talked more and decided we would all go to the barbecue. I was nervous. I didn't know how Real would look at me after what happen at the club. Sha dropped Angie off at home, and she and I went back to her house.

"So, I'll be out your hair in two days, sweetie," I said, hoping I wouldn't be a burden on Sha.

"Bitch, you're my sister. Why would you even sweat it? You can always come here, and don't forget that."

We talked and watched movies. Sha dozed off, so I went into the guest bedroom and realized that I never brought my clothes in. I got the clothes out of my trunk that I would need for a few days. I didn't want to have to pack all over again. I checked my phone and had twelve missed calls some from my mom, Benz, and Mel. I knew Mel must've called and told them what happened. I didn't want to deal with my mom, but I wanted to get it over with. I called my mother, and we talked for three hours straight.

I called Mel to see why he called my mother making it seem like the chick was texting him just to start some shit. That's not even how the shit went down, and he knew it.

"Hello, Nel, are you okay?" Mel asked.

"Oh, I will be. Why the fuck you call my mom, selling her that fake bullshit? You know damn well what you did, so be a man and confess that shit!" I screamed into the phone.

"Nel, can you please come back home so we can talk? I'm gon' keep it one hundred and put the shit out there. Just please come and talk to me, Nel. Please?"

"That's not my home anymore motherfucker, but I'll come so we can talk. Just so we are clear, Mel…it's over between us." I hung up the phone and made my way back over to Mel's crib.

I just wanted to know who this bitch was. It really didn't matter, but I needed the closure.

Jamel

I was waiting patiently for Nel to arrive. I felt a little better that I had the chance to talk to her. I didn't know what I was going to tell her when she got here, but staying together would be the main topic.

Nel pulled up to the house. She sat in the car for what seem like forever. I opened the door, and she walked up the steps. She was wearing those sexy jeans I liked, and I wanted my girl back. She walked past me and sat down on the sofa that was for one person so she wouldn't have to sit next to me. I closed the door and noticed the look in her eyes; she was hurt. Nel was such a strong person, but I knew I went too far.

"Nel, baby, please don't do this. Please don't leave me. I can't live without you," I cried out.

"Mel. I didn't come over here for that shit. You said you were keeping it one hundred and if you don't start talking, I'm out!"

"Nel, I am keeping it one hundred. You being in my life is what I need, don't leave me now, not like this let's work this out."

Nel looked at me like I was her worst enemy.

"Jamel, you hurt me like no one has ever fucking hurt me before. You cheated, and you put off spending time with your woman to be with some jump off bitch. You can't expect me to stay. Now, if I was one of those bitches, I would think the problem was me, but, honey, it's you. Any man would be glad to have me from cooking his breakfast, washing his draw, fucking him every night, to having his back when no one else does! So for you to play me, that shit hurt my fucking soul. So, why cheat? What was so great about the bitch that you had to cheat?"

"I fucked up, Nel. I know, but I just got caught up with the street life. Baby, I'm sorry. I fucked this bitch once or twice, and I didn't think I would regret it, but I did. That's how I knew I love you more than anything."

"So, this bitch you fucked…you only fucked her once or twice… which one is it?"

"Yes, Nel. I swear, it was only twice. She was the only one, baby, and I'm sorry. I'll never do that shit again. Please don't leave me, Nel. I can't breathe without you."

"Well, Mel, I don't know what to say, but it's over. I gave you all of me…all of me. You are all I know. You were my first everything, and you played me. I'm hurt, and I always thought you were the one to take my pain away. Now…you're the cause of it."

Nel started crying. That shit hurt like hell to see her cry because of me.

"Nel, baby, please don't cry. I can fix this; I can take the pain away. Baby, please just let me make things right between us. I promise you I'll make it right." Nel cried and let me comfort her.

"Mel, you hurt me. baby." Was the only thing she could manage to say between tears. We fell asleep in each other arms.

Chanel

I woke up, and Mel was still sleeping. I felt sick and hated that I allowed him to suck me back in. I couldn't take him back. I knew it was more to him cheating with that one bitch. I needed to know the truth. I knew that we could probably have worked it out, but it was too far gone. I needed to make an appointment at the salon. That's where all the gossip comes from. I will go and get my hair touched up and talk to my girl, Sonto, who really is a male, but he's gay.

I got up and went into what used to be our room. I looked around and thought about the good times we had. I felt stupid for still being at Mel's house, but I knew that love just didn't go away right away. I was eventually going to leave but right now, it feels good that he was crying for me to stay. I knew it was all an act. I didn't know what to do and every time I thought about it, I started crying. My cell phone vibrated, startling me. I looked down and notice it was Sha.

"Hello? Nel, I've been calling you for the last hour where are you?"

"I'm at Mel's. He wanted to talk, but I'm leaving in a second. Don't worry. Everything's okay," I told Sha.

"Okay. Well, I was just checking on you. El asked if I wanted to come over and chill for a minute. I'll be home later. Did you grab the key I left out earlier?" she asked.

"Yes, I got it. I'll see you soon. Bye, boo."

Sha hung up, and I decided it was time for me to go. I didn't want to, but I needed space and being around Mel was too much for me right now.

"Mel, I'm leaving. I'll see you around," I said as I grabbed my purse.

"Nel, wait. Where are you going? I thought we were going to work this out, baby."

"Mel, I never said that; you did. I need some space. Things aren't going to be better overnight," I said, opening up the house door.

"Okay, Nel, I can give you space because I love you. Can I get a hug before you leave?"

I tried walking past him, but he grabbed and hugged me. "I love you, Nel...more than anything."

"Bye, Mel. And please don't blow my phone up. Just leave me alone. okay?" I said pulling away from him.

Jamel

I didn't want to stay in an empty house. This would've been my last day at work before I went on a six-week vacation, but I called my boy, Aaron, and told him I couldn't work because of a personal issue. I know them niggas mad. They were going hard on that mixtape, but I couldn't right now.

I couldn't put in my vacation at the same time as Nel because I was going to my boy's wedding this Saturday, so I had to wait until the following week, I didn't want to at the time anyway because that way when she went back to work I would be off, and she wouldn't bother me with that quality time shit. But now that the shit hit the fan, I gotta get out of the doghouse. I will be kissing ass to get my back in good. I would be leaving Friday morning for my boy's bachelor's party.

I decided to just chill and call RJ, Money, and Cruz to blow one. I haven't spoken to Cruz in a while. None of the girls like Cruz because he was always telling RJ and I that being faithful is for weak ass niggas. Angie overheard and told Nel and Sha what he said. I called them up and was glad Nel kept the house clean so I wouldn't have to worry about that for now at least. I waited until they arrived.

"Yo', fool, you should keep your door locked at all times you don't know who coming for your ass," Cruz joked as he walked into my house

"Well, people that got some sense knock before they come in somebody house!" I said as I gave my boy a dab.

"What up with y'all?" I said to Money and RJ

"Shit, ready for this loud," RJ said as he bounced his head listening to the music Cruz just turned on my PlayStation 4.

"Aye, fool, turn that shit down. Your ass get out the house and don't know how to act," I laughed.

"Man, y'all know that nigga was in the dog house. Jessica ass found out he got that white bitch pregnant and his ass been on lockdown for a while," Money laughed.

"Man, fuck y'all niggas. This nigga the one single now. His girl left his ass and shit," Cruz said.

"Shit, her ass just left. She ain't going nowhere. I'm giving my girl space to get her mind right, that's all," I said, feeling confident my girl was coming back to me.

"What you mean get her mind right?" Money asked.

"Aye, check this, she hurting right now. That's all, but when she find out I'm still that nigga… plus, I'm her first love…she ain't going nowhere."

"Oh yeah, you think shit sweet?" Money asked.

"Man, I know what I got to do to keep my baby. Besides, she can't replace me. I'm that nigga."

Cruz sat down and started talking. "Man, fuck her. Stop sweating just one bitch you got Candy's ass and that other bitch I seen you with, and I'm not a Christian but God, she got blessed in all the right places."

"Man, sit down before Jessica come beating your ass again," Money said and everyone started laughing.

"Oh shit, that bachelor party this weekend, ain't it?" Money asked referring to our boy E.

"Hell yeah! I can't wait. I know Benz 'bout to have ass shaking everywhere for his boy too," Cruz said as he rolled up a blunt.

"Aye, RJ, you rolling with us? We can't leave you back here with the women alone you can't survive with all three?" Money joked.

"Shit, hell yeah, might as well," RJ said back.

We started taking turns playing the video game, and put the blunt into rotation.

Sha

I pulled up to El's spot. I thought he had a nice house from the outside. The landscape looked really nice. I walked up to the door and rang the doorbell. El opened the door before I could even blink.

"Hey, baby, come in," El said.

"The outside doesn't do your house justice," I said, looking around his house. "How many bedrooms do you have?" I asked.

"I have six and a den," he responded.

He brought me into the living room and some nigga was sitting on the couch, talking on the phone.

"Yeah and my package better be on its way," I heard El's boy say.

When I sat on the couch across from him, I knew who it was. *Damn he look like T.I.* I thought to myself.

"Aye man, you remember, Sha, I was telling you about," El said to Real.

"Yes, what up, gorgeous? Good seeing you again," Real said as he smiled.

"Hi," was all I could say back.

"Don't be acting all shy now," El joked.

"Aye, baby, I'm gon' blow this loud with this nigga real quick then you'll have me all to yourself," El said.

"Okay, cool," I laughed at him.

Real started rolling up and within minutes they were in rotation. El asked if I smoke, and I said no.

"So, is your girl just as beautiful as you are in the light," Real asked.

"Oh, of course. I fucks with nothing but them pretty bitches," I laughed and so did they.

"Yeah, I like her man she cool," Real said.

"So, I hear you're in love with my girl," I laughed, looking at El.

"I know El told you that, but nawl, I don't know her like that, but I most def would like to get to know her. El big mouth also told me she done with ol' boy, Mel."

"Yeah, but that's something you going to have to discuss with her because I don't put my sister business out like that."

"I can understand that. You real, and that's what up," Real said as he shook his head looking at El.

"But, can you tell her to call me? We can be friends nothing extra until she falls in love with a nigga," Real said smoking the last of the blunt.

"Now I see why y'all cool, El said the same thing to me, I guess great minds think alike," I smiled.

"No baby great minds think for themselves," Real said as he looked at his phone.

"Please have her call. I can be that shoulder she need or ear to listen, I'm not a bad guy." Real smiled.

"No you're not," I agreed with him.

We chatted for a while longer, and I promised to have Nel call him. He finally left and I enjoyed his company, but I was happy he left so El and I could talk.

I move to the couch Real sat on so I could be across from El.

"You're so handsome," I smiled at him.

"Girl, don't start that flirting," he laughed and moved to the couch I was sitting on. "So, how you feel about me," El asked, looking in my eyes.

"Well, I really like you. You're sweet, you keep me laughing, and I can tell you're very genuine," I said as I stared back at him.

"Can you see yourself being with me in a relationship?" he asked.

"Yes, but with time. I'm really just getting over um...my— I paused, looking away.

"I told you to always look me in the eyes. You don't have to turn away. Don't feel like you have to hide anything from me. Who is it? Your baby's father that you're getting over?" he said.

"Yes, and I'm over him. It's just we've been through a lot. Our relationship didn't necessarily end bad, I just left him because he put the streets before me, and things just went left," I said happy to finally break the tension I felt.

"So, are you guys working on getting back together or what?"

"No, we're just being good parents. I mean, he wants to, but I don't," I said, looking in his eyes wanting to kiss him.

"Okay. Well, I can trust that. You smell so good." He pulled me

104

closer. "I like you, Sha-Sha. I really do."

"I like you too, Elvin."

"Damn, why did I tell this woman my name?" he joked.

"Oh, so I can't call you that?" I said as I licked my lips. He finally grabbed and kissed my lips.

"You can call me whatever, baby," he said between kisses. He was hard as fuck, but it was too soon for all of that

"Man, I want you so bad," El blurted out.

"You? I haven't had sex since last October."

"Damn, and you still breathing? I can't go no longer than…" he paused.

"It's okay. I know you're getting yours. We're not in a relationship, but please tell me you practice safe sex?" I said as I looked into his eyes.

"Oh, hell yeah. Only wifey can get this dick raw," he said as he pointed at his hard dick.

"You are so crazy," I laughed.

"So, how long are we talking about me waiting?" he asked.

"At least a month if things are still going this smooth," I answered.

"Well, I can wait, but I don't know, girl. You keep trying to feel on me and shit," El teased me.

"Oh, whatever. I am not. If I wanted to touch you, I would like this," I said as I pressed my hand across his pants where I felt his dick.

"Sha, you better stop before something happened up in here."

"Something like what?" I said and kissed him.

"Something like this."

He lifted my sun dress up and slid my panties to the side in slid his tongue along my juice box.

"Umm that feels so good, oh yes."

"You like that?" He asked working his tongue like magic.

"Yes, I like that, Elvin. Yes."

He sucked and licked and sucked some more until I came all on his face.

I sat up and kissed him. I wanted him bad, but Ms. Glory taught us girls to hold out on the cookie jar for as long as we could. Ms. Glory also said if he wanted to tasted the cookie, to let him. Ms. Glory had a lot of men remedies.

"Why you smiling so hard for? That nut must've felt like heaven," he said, pulling me onto his lap.

"It did," I laughed back.

"What am I'm going to do with you?" he asked.

El started to tickle me but stopped when my cell phone vibrated. I sat up and saw that it was Benz. I didn't want to answer, but El said take the call while he washed his face. I guess he saw my screen.

"Hello," I said as I watched El leave the room to go upstairs.

"Hey. Dang, we can't get a call saying 'hello, family,'" Benz joked.

"Right," I laughed. "Where is my baby?" I waited until Junior got on the phone.

"Hi, Mommy. Why you didn't call me, Mama? You mean."

I had to laugh. Benz was teaching him all kind of shit over there.

"Mommy's been busy, baby. I was gon' call you. What have you been doing all day?" I asked my son.

"Me and daddy went out to eat, daddy got my bike, and I got two games, and I got my money up today."

"Benz, I know you got me on speaker. What have you been exposing my baby to?" I laughed.

"Man, I don't know where he got that from," he said as he got on the phone.

"What up, though? I heard about what happen between sis and Mel. She cool?"

I saw El coming in the room. This time, he sat on the other couch.

"Yeah, she cool. She's just hurt. Mel was foul for that shit, but I'll call my son back later kiss him for me," I said and glanced over at El who was looking at the T.V.

"Only if you kiss me when I see you."

"Boy, please! Bye."

"Damn, you funny acting. I can't wait to get to my pussy. You been keeping it warm for me, haven't you?"

I smiled because that used to have a major effect on me when he said that. I looked over at El, who was looking at me in a lustful kind of way.

"Okay. Well, I'll call you guys later, and quit teaching my baby that shit," I laughed before we hung up. "I'm sorry about that El," I said.

"You don't have to apologize for talking to your son or your son's father."

I smiled and sat on his lap and kissed him once again.

"I better get going. It's getting late."

"Oh, you get your nut and run?" he laughed.

"Oh, shut up," I said. I grabbed my purse to get ready to leave.

El wrapped his arms around my waist.

"Sha, can you stay the night with me?" he asked.

"So, you could have your way with me? I'll pass," I laughed, turning around and hugging him.

"No, so you could have your way with me," he said, caressing my back.

"You're something else," I laughed, sneaking another kiss before he walked me to my car.

"Drive safe, baby. Call me when you make it home."

I drove home in lust. I was happy, and I wished I could have the moment for life. When I got home, I noticed Nel was back. I almost forgot my girl was staying with me.

"Hey, girl. You're glowing. Let me find out you gave El some," Nel teased as I walked in.

"No, but he ate my pussy, and it felt so good. Right after he finished, Benz called. You talking about feeling awkward, Nel, OMG! I guess El seen my screen, and you know I got Benz under baby daddy? Well, El was all like go ahead and answer while I wash my face, and I'm talking to Benz, and you know Benz ass talking about am I keeping his pussy warm for him. That's when El walked back in the room."

"Girl, Benz's ass is crazy. Could El hear him talking? Did Benz hear El talking? What happen next?"

"Nel, this is not an episode of *Love and Hip-Hop*. Girl, calm down. El was sitting across from me on another couch, and he didn't say anything until I got off the phone," I said, sitting down.

"Nel, it feels like I've cheated on Benz when we're not even together." I'm tired of Benz having an effect on my life."

"That's because you still care about Benz. That's your baby's father, but if you guys not meant to be and you don't want to be with him, you better let Benz know because he thinks your pussy is still his," Nel laughed and so did I.

"Girl, you right, but El is just so smooth. Guess what, bitch?" I said, getting hyped up.

"What?" Nel said as she turned the chicken in the skillet she was cooking.

"Real was there, and we kicked it for a minute. He asked me to have you call him."

"What?" She looked at me.

"Girl, yes. I guess El told him about you and Mel breaking up, and he said if you need a shoulder to lean on or an ear to listen to call him."

"Well, that's sweet, but Real is too much for me. He's a little too real for me," she laughed.

"I think you should. I mean, not to get back at Mel, but a male friend wouldn't hurt, remember Drey ass? He was our best male friend until he got a girlfriend and dissed us," I laughed.

"Girl, yes. That was our boy. I miss him."

"Me too. He always kept it real with us if we were dressed like some hoes. We would go change until he said we looked like some sexy women."

"Girl, yes. I remember that shit," she laughed.

"How did my boo look? Was he still looking like T.I in the daylight?"

"Man, y'all made for each other. He asked me the same about you," I shook my head.

"Girl, and you know T.I is my celebrity husband?"

"Yeah, but do T.I know is the question?" I teased.

"Bitch, boo."

"Did you eat over there? Well, I know he ate, but did you?" Nel laughed and turned to look at me.

"Bitch, shut up and no, I didn't, so fix me a plate. I want to get catered to in my house for once."

"Bitch, you lucky I love you." Nel fixed our plates. We ate, laughed, and talked about El and Real.

"Well, I'll have to see what's good with him at the barbecue before I call him. Damn, bitch, I just thought about it. I threw his number down in the club after we left because Mel was tripping."

"Well, you'll see him at the barbecue. Get it then, or I can have El get it," I said, getting up to help Nel clean up the kitchen.

"No, I'll wait until Friday because I might change my mind if he's there with his girlfriend."

"Bitch, go on. The way that nigga checking for you, he better not have a girl," I laughed, but I was serious.

"Well, we will see," she said.

We cleaned the kitchen and made our way to bed. Nel slept in the guest bedroom, and she loved how the bed was extra soft just like she liked it.

Nel

I just got the keys to my condo. Angie and Sha were shopping all afternoon the day before for furniture, wall décor, candles, and everything I thought to buy. RJ drove the moving truck over to Mel's to finish getting the rest of my things. I wasn't taking any of the appliances or electronics. I just had way too many clothes. Once we made it to the Mel's house, RJ got out to get my things.

"Hey, what's up, man?" Mel said. putting the stopper in the screen door so it would stay open.

"Shit, about to get Nel's clothes. If she's anything like her sister, I know she has a lot of them," RJ joked, walking into the house.

"And let's not forget the shoes. She has so many damn shoes," Mel joked back.

"Hey! Mel," Sha said as she walked past Mel.

"What's up, girl?" Mel looked at me.

"Hey," I tried to walked past him.

"Nel, you don't have to spend money on rent. You could've just stayed here in the other room. I promise I would've gave you space until you was ready to work things out."

I don't know why he assumed I was coming back.

"Look, Mel, let's not do this. I have a paper due tomorrow. I need to get settled at home, so I can put the finishing touches on it."

"Okay, but before you leave, come holler at me around back please," he said, walking to the backyard.

"Oh, so you can't help me get my stuff?"

"I don't want you to leave, Nel. Why would I help you leave me?"

I couldn't answer that, so I just walked into the house and gathered my stuff so I could leave.

We finished packing everything I owned into the truck, and RJ drove the truck back over to my condo with Sha, so I could talk this last talk with Mel.

"So, you really leaving me?" Mel asked, listening to me walk up on him and sitting on the swing in the backyard. It was those type of swings that old folks would have in their backyard with one long seat made out of wood. I begged Mel to make me one and he did.

"Mel, what you expect me to do? Stay and not be able to trust you?"

"I don't know, Nel, but leaving me shouldn't be an option," he yelled.

I never saw him this pissed when talking to me or even arguing with me.

"What you mean part of the plan, so cheating on me and me staying and dealing with your shit is? No, Jamel, you got life fucked up, and you on some bullshit. I thought coming back here to make amends with you would settle things. Yes, I'm leaving because of you. None of this is my fault. I told you from the time we got together in high school if you ever played me, I would leave your ass. Just because we have history now don't change shit. I have no tolerance for cheating and out of all people, your ass should know that. You helped my family get over what my dad did to my mother and us. Why would you do that to me after what I been through?"

"Nel, it's not always about you. Why do you think the world revolves around your ass?"

"Mel, fuck you, and have a nice life." I walked away.

"See what I mean? You always running from your problems to let the next person deal with them," Mel walked behind me until I stopped in my tracks.

"What are you saying? None of this makes sense. You have nothing bad to say about me, so you're making shit up. How is it my fault? You cheated not me. I did everything a woman is supposed to do for her man, and you know what? I don't want to leave on a bad note. We probably can't be friends right now, but maybe one day we could."

"Friends? Yeah right, Nel. You're more to me than just a friend. I can't get over you. Yes, I fucked up. Yes, I'm making shit up because I don't know what else to do. The woman I'm supposed to be marrying next year is leaving me."

"What, Mel?" I looked at him.

"I said the woman I'm supposed to marry next year is leaving me."

"Mel, you were going to ask me to marry you?"

"I mean…yeah. Eventually I was."

I didn't know if he was just trying to say anything to get me to stay or what, but I thought about the message from the chick he fucked and made up my mind right then and there.

"Mel, I'm sorry, but I can't keep doing this with you. You playing with my feelings is messed up, but it's cool, Mel. Stay up, and I will always love you, but we can't be together, Mel. I'm sorry." This time I walked away, and he didn't stop me.

I was putting my clothes together and glad Sha and Angie helped. Even though Angie had to stay late at work, she still wanted to come over so she could help me. It was now 5:30 pm, and there were still clothes that needed to be hung up. It would have to wait until later in the week. I had to finish my paper. It was due tomorrow at 9:00 am, and I wasn't about to be up all night even though I just had a couple more things to add to my paper, I still wanted to submit it tonight before I went to bed. Sha and Angie left for the day.

I really liked how my condo looked. I didn't have to compromise about how I wanted my house to look because this was my shit. I took a hot bath before finishing up my paper.

When I finished, I double checked everything before I submitted it online into my teacher's mailbox. I looked at the time, and it was just 9:40 pm. I was hungry but didn't have much food. I needed to get groceries. I thought about it and knew I would be hungry in the morning if I didn't do it tonight and besides, I thought it was best to grocery shop at night.

I took my pajamas off and put on my grey leggings that read

PINK down the side from Victoria's Secret. I threw on the matching hoodie and quickly pulled my hair into a ponytail, grabbed my purse, cell phone, and keys, and left for the store.

While driving, I tried to keep my emotions together. I was so hurt. I felt like I could just die, but I knew if my mother could do it, I had to also. I decided to just head to Wal-Mart since it was the closest to my condo. I would only grab a few things because I hated carrying groceries in the house, which usually was Mel's Job.

I went to frozen aisle and grabbed my favorite cookie dough ice cream. I turned around to go on the next aisle to grab some water bottles. I was trying to reach them, but it was up to high. I jumped, trying to pull it toward the edge so I could grab it.

"Need some help?" a male's voice said from behind me. I turned around and was shocked to see that it was Real.

"Chanel?" Real smiled.

"Real?" I said back.

"Wow, you're even more beautiful from when we met in the club."

I just stared at him like he was really the rapper T.I. He was so sexy.

"Is this the one you want?" Real asked, grabbing the water from the top shelf.

"Thank you. I think I almost had it," I choked on my words.

"Man, I can't believe I ran into you. I've been talking about you all day," Real confessed.

"You have?" I said.

"Well, earlier to your homegirl."

"Oh yeah, she told me. I was just busy moving and finishing my paper for school."

"It's cool. I figured you might've been busy."

"Well, yeah. I should get going. It's getting late, and I hate carrying groceries in," I stated, turning around.

"Oh, okay. Well, I could help you if you want?"

"No, I'm fine. Thanks, though."

"Okay. Well, can you call me when you get home so I know you made it alright?"

"Yes, but I will need your number again. I lost the card you gave me."

Real wasted no time pulling out his business card. He watched me like a hawk, and I was nervous.

I grabbed the card, thanked him again, and made my way to the register. I wondered if he was out shopping for a woman because he had Slim Fast bars and protein shakes, something usually a woman would buy. It was only one line open, so he let me go first.

When I was done, he said bye, and I made my way to my car. I was glad it was cool out because I was hot as hell in there for some reason. When I finished, I looked around, and he was parked two rows ahead of me. Next thing I knew, he walked toward me, and I couldn't help but to admire his swag. His walk was even sexy.

"So, you got everything in okay?" he asked, looking at me. I wondered if he noticed how nervous I was.

"Yes, I did. Thanks. Well, I'll call you when I get in, okay?"

"I'll be waiting, gorgeous," he grabbed my hand and kissed it.

"You're sweet," I got into my car.

On the ride home, I was smiling from ear to ear. Besides my girls, I didn't remember the last time having something to smile about.

Once I got home and inside, I finished putting my groceries away and fixed a quick snack. It was now 11:15 pm. I brushed my teeth, washed my face, put my pajamas back on, and laid down in my soft bed. I'd had a long day. I was about to call Real when I dozed off to sleep.

I woke up to my phone ringing. I looked at the clock in it was 3:20 am.

"Hello! I said in a raspy, sleepy voice.

"Hey, Chanel. Are you okay?"

"Yes, who is this?"

"It's Real. Remember you said you'll call when you got home so that I knew you made it home safe?"

"Real, I am so sorry! I fell asleep. I was planning on calling you. I promise!" I felt bad he must've thought something happened to me.

"It's cool. I just wanted to make sure you were okay."

"Did Sha give you my number?"

"No, she didn't, but promise me you won't get mad when I tell you how I got your number?" Real laughed.

"I promise," I laughed back.

"You remember when you dropped your cell phone that night at the club, and I handed it to you?" Real said.

"Yeah, I remember," I smiled.

"Well, I called my number from your phone so I would have your number, and I erased it from your call log."

I was quiet for a minute until I busted out laughing.

"Oh, wow! Yeah, you are bold, I can't believe you did that. What if my boyfriend—" I started to say but stopped.

"Well, if your boyfriend at the time what?" he asked.

"Nothing. Anyway I am fine Real, I made it home safe."

"Okay, so that lil' problem out your hair I see." Real asked.

"Yeah, something like that, so I guess Sha told you about the break-up, huh?" I asked.

"Well, to be honest, your girl didn't feel it would be right talking about your situation to me. My boy, El, did but that's because I kept asking about you when he told me he was kicking it with your homegirl."

"Oh, okay. Well, yeah there you have it."

"So, can I call you tomorrow so we could talk and maybe do lunch or even dinner…if that's okay with you?" Real asked.

"I don't know, Real. I'm just getting out of a relationship. I think it's too soon to be dating," I yawned.

"We'll look at it as two friends eating out then," Real suggested.

"Um, I guess that's okay as long as we both agree it's not a date?"

"Yeah, girl, it's not a date," Real laughed.

"Okay, well let's do lunch because dinner sounds more like a date," I joked.

"Whatever makes you happy, beautiful."

"Good night, Real."

"Good night, beautiful," Real hung up.

I had to admit, I was kind of happy. Even though I felt it was too soon, I needed something to ease the pain in my heart. Besides, it was only lunch. I thought about work and didn't want to return next week. I would call tomorrow and get the third week off like I planned at first but decided not to at the last minute. Besides, the intern that was taking my place was happy to be getting the experience.

Angie

$\mathcal{I}$ got up early to make RJ some breakfast. He talked about going to the bachelor party last night on Friday with Money and Mel. I trusted RJ, so I didn't have a problem with it. RJ has been doing a lot better. He was going into business with Gary, and they already built RJ some great client lists. I was happy things were going good with RJ and I, but I was still missing something, and I didn't know what that was.

"Bae, breakfast is ready!" I yelled upstairs.

"Here I come now, baby," RJ ran downstairs like a big ass kid. He ran over to me, picked me up, and kissed me.

"I love you so much, girl!"

"I love you more, baby." I pulled away to fix his plate.

"Well if you love daddy so much, do me a favor?"

"What's that? I am not going to bend over this counter RJ. Didn't you get enough this morning?" I laughed.

"Girl, I can never get enough of that pussy, but I need you to go to the mall and grab a few things for me. I don't know what to wear to no wedding."

"Boy, I hope you know what to wear to ours," I laughed and placed his plate of food in front of him.

"I know to wear a tux," he laughed, stuffing his mouth with bacon.

"I got you, baby. How much of a sign on bonus did Gary give you? I need a pair of shoes for my service?"

RJ laughed at me.

"Girl, you nosey, but go ahead grab you some shoes, a dress, or whatever you like."

"Yay!" I jumped up and down. I could buy my own clothing with my own money, but something about spending your man's money is always better.

I took a shower and a quick nap. When I woke up, I told RJ I was heading to the mall because he was leaving tomorrow morning. I tried calling Nel, but she wasn't answering her phone, so I called Sha.

"Hey, Angie. What's up? Sha said into the phone.

"Girl, I'm heading to the mall and wanted you and Nel to go with me."

"I'm down, but Nel hasn't called me back. I called my twice," she mentioned.

"Yeah, I just called. Maybe she stayed up all night to finish that paper. I'll stop by her house and see if she's still asleep. If so, I'll just let her sleep and come get you."

"Okay, boo," she said.

I headed over to my sister's. When I got there, Nel's car was there, so I knew she was still sleeping, I used the spare key she gave me and let myself in. I looked around the house. Everything was so nice. I made my way upstairs to Nel's room. When I peeked in Nel's room, she was sleeping like a baby. I didn't want to disturb her, so I left just as quietly as I came. It was now 12:30 in the afternoon. I picked up Sha and headed to the mall.

While Sha and I were shopping, Nel texted us and said she just got up and she'd call us later. I was done shopping for R.J, and I was becoming hungry.

"I think he should be good with the stuff I just got him," I laughed.

"Men should know not to send their girls to shop for them. We buy way more than they need," Sha laughed.

"Okay, let's go grab something for this barbecue tomorrow. I ain't trying to be out dressed by them duck bitches that's gon' be there," I joked.

"Bitch, please, even on your baddest days, those bitches couldn't look better than you."

We shopped a little longer before we called it quits.

"Man, I'm hungry what time is it?" Sha asked me.

"It's almost 2:20," I answered.

"Let's go to that sandwich shop. I want a grilled cheese and tomato soup," she said.

We put our bags in my car and headed over to the shop. When we walked in, it was really packed. We had to wait ten minutes for a table. I noticed Nel and Real sitting down.

"Bitch, look at this. You ain't going to believe this shit!" I looked at Nel and Real.

"What, bitch?" Sha followed my eyes.

"Angie, that is not Nel and that nigga, Real?" Sha asked

"Wow, yes it is. Y'all bitches keeping secrets!" I said pissed they didn't tell me.

"I didn't know nothing about this. I swear, Angie," Sha said.

"Let's walk over there and say hi," I said.

We walked over, and Nel had her back facing us. Real glanced in our direction and smiled. I guess a little too hard because Nel turned around.

"Well, well, well what do we have here?" Sha asked.

"Hi, girls....I texted you guys, but I overslept," Nel confessed

Sha and I just stared at Nel for a brief minute not knowing what to say next.

"Good afternoon, ladies?" Real spoke, breaking the silence between us.

"Hey, Real," Sha spoke.

"Hey, nice to see you again, Real," I said.

"Wow, I feel like a schoolgirl on a date that just got caught by my mom," Nel joked.

"Oh, we're sorry. We just wanted to come and speak, that's all," Sha said.

The waiter told Sha and I that our table was ready which was right in front of Nel's table. We sat down and ordered our food. We talked small talk but not too loud. We were trying to listen to Nel and Real's conversation. We overheard their whole conversation.

Sha and I were getting up to leave because I had to get back and pack RJ's bag.

"It was nice seeing you again, Real, and Nel, we'll meet you later on I guess. The guys are leaving for the bachelor's party in the morning." I looked at Nel.

"It was a pleasure," Real smiled.

"Hey, what day is the wedding on?" Nel asked.

"I believe Saturday, but you know the bachelor party is Friday and them niggas gon' clown, but just call us later, boo. Bye, Real," I said, and we walked off.

Sha decided to go over my house because we wanted to get the details from Nel at the same time.

"I cannot believe that bitch," Sha laughed.

"I know right? Who would have thought? I was sure she was going to go back to Mel's ass. Nel is so sneaky. I can't wait until she calls," I said as I pulled up in my driveway and noticed Mel's car.

"Oh shit, Mel's here. Now he's going to ask where is Nel. We got to say something," I said.

"I got this," Sha said with a smile.

We walked in and sure enough, Mel was there looking like he lost his best friend.

"Hey, Angie. Hey, Sha," he said and looked at the door, probably wondering where Nel was at.

"Hey, Mel. How are you?" I asked.

"Well, I would be better if I had my girl, but since that's not happening right now, I'm maintaining."

"Oh, ok. Well, take care of yourself," I walked past Mel to RJ and gave RJ a kiss.

RJ hugged me and spoke to Sha.

"Hey, where your girl?" Mel asked Sha.

"Oh, she getting her condo together," Sha lied, looking at me.

"Oh, okay. Cool," Mel said

"Well, we're going to go pack your things, baby, and you guys better behave tomorrow," I said to RJ.

"Girl, you know I always do," RJ laughed at me.

We walked upstairs to pack RJ's things and waited for Nel's call. We heard the doorbell ring and thought it could be for the guys since Nel hadn't called yet. We peeped toward the steps only to find out it was only Money.

"Yo', Yo', what y'all niggas doing?" Money asked, sitting on my fluffy couch.

"Shit, nigga, you packed for tomorrow?" Mel asked Money.

"Nigga, hell naw. I got all night for that, but I need to. I don't know what to wear for the wedding. Shit, I'm more hyped about the bachelor's party," Money said.

"Shit, who you telling?" Mel agreed.

Sha and I were still eaves dropping and shaking our heads. Money didn't have a girl, so he was in the clear, but Mel shouldn't be worried about any party that's why his ass single now.

"Girl, can you believe that nigga? I swear, I hope Nel don't go back to his ass. He be fronting when really he just hate the fact his ass got caught up," Sha said and looked at me.

"Let's hope she doesn't either. The nigga did a 360 from when they first got together, but shit, niggas can't appreciate a good woman until she's gone," I said.

"Shit, or replaced because if Real is smooth like El, it's over for Mel's ass," Sha laughed.

Nel

*R*eal waited at the table for me to come back from the restroom.

"We've been here a long time," I sat down.

"Yeah, but I just want to get to know you better. You told me a lot, but I still want to know more," Real said as he looked at me.

"Well, ask away," I said.

"So, I know your age and birthday. What's your favorite color?" he asked.

"Green and brown. Don't ask why either. How old are you? You haven't let me ask you any questions yet." I said as I looked at him.

"I'm twenty-six. I'll be twenty-seven on Friday," he said.

"Well, happy early birthday," I smiled.

"You don't have any kids with ol' boy, do you?" he asked.

"No, I'm not ready for kids, and thank God I don't have them with him," I said as I played with my leftover food with my fork.

I gave Real a run down on my relationship with Mel. I felt comfortable talking to him for some reason.

"Why do they call you Real, and what is your real name?" I asked, thinking he was so sexy.

"They call me Real because I am the realist you will ever meet by far."

"Okay. So, you just keep it real at all times, no little white lies, and no mistakes?" I asked.

"I don't need to lie and yes, everyone makes mistakes. Mistakes made me the man I am today," Real said as touched my hand.

"What is your real name? You didn't answer that question." I laughed and pulled my hand back because his touch did something to me.

"My real name is Leon, and don't be telling people my name, girl, that's classified information only," he laughed.

"That's cute, Leon. That name fits you," I said, smiling at him.

"So, is this what friends do because I feel like we're on a date?" Real asked as he grabbed my hand again.

"Yes, friends do, and we discussed this yesterday; we're just two friends out having lunch, Real. You know that."

"Look, I'm gon' be upfront. I'm cool with being friends, getting to know each other, but I'm also going to make you fall in love with me," Real said still holding my hand.

I just stared into his eyes. *Could you really find your soulmate on one date, even if you just got out of a long-term relationship?* I thought to myself.

"Nel, you hear me. What if you fall in love with me, and I fall for you? What would that be called?" Real asked, looking back into my eyes with smirk on his face.

"I don't know, Real. I guess if I do fall in love, we will cross that bridge when we get there."

"So, we can be friends and if you fall in love, we can move forward with the next step?"

I didn't want to answer that. I just broke up with my high school sweetheart less than a week ago. I had to admit, Real was a good distraction but mentally, I just wasn't ready.

"I don't want to answer that now, Real," I said.

"Okay, I'm sorry. I just know that I like you and as time goes by, spending more time with you will only make me want you more."

Real put his finger up to my chin to lifted my head up because I was looking down.

"Okay, but you know my situation. Let's just work on a friendship first, please," I said, looking at him and hoping he wouldn't push me further.

"Okay, Nel. I'm sorry. Are you ready to go?" he asked

"Sure, but I have to ask who were you buying SlimFast bars and protein shakes for at the store that day?" He started laughing at me.

"You're very observant, Chanel. I like that, but it was for my mother sweetie. I don't have a woman, if that's what you're hinting at," he smiled, and I just laughed at myself.

Real paid for our lunch, and we walked out together.

"Damn!" I heard Real say from behind me.

"What?" I asked as I turned around facing him.

"Nothing!" he smirked at me.

"I umm…had a great time, friend. I would like to see you again if that's cool with you?" I said.

"You know I want to see your ass. Don't play games," Real laughed.

"Okay, cool," I smiled.

"So, what are you about to get into?" Real asked.

"I guess go home. I got to go find the girls. I didn't tell them about our lunch date, so when they saw me they were a little shock," I laughed.

"Yeah, I noticed that. They gon' question you like crazy when you see them, and I noticed you said lunch date."

"Okay, Real, if you want to call it a date, then it was a date," I pushed him against the car.

"Yo', keep your hands to yourself. You couldn't help but touch me," he teased.

"Boy, please. You know you like me touching you."

"That I do. Matter of fact, do it again," he laughed.

"You're crazy. You know that?" I started laughing, trying to hide the fact I was blushing.

"So, what you doing tomorrow? You going to that wedding you and your girls was talking about earlier?" Real asked.

"Oh, yeah. I am," I lied. I didn't want to tell him El invited me and Angie to his barbecue. I wanted to see if he had a lil' boo, and how *real* he really was.

"Oh, okay then…damn…cool. Maybe Saturday, if you're free, we could go see a movie," he mentioned.

"Sure, we could do that if my Friday goes okay."

"Okay, well, I might just sleep through Friday so Saturday could come faster," he said as he came closer toward me.

"Boy, what am I going to do with you?" I smiled, taking in his cologne.

"Don't even ask me anything like that," he joked.

"You're right. I forgot who I was talking to. Here, give me a hug so I can go. Thanks for the talk," I said as I hugged him.

"Okay, drive safe, C," he said, giving me a nickname.

"Bye, Leon," I said.

"That shit sound so sexy rolling off your tongue," he said as he bit the bottom of his lip.

We both left, and I was kind of happy to spend time with him. He was actually good company and so sexy.

I called Sha, and she was still at Angie's House. I was a little nervous because I knew the girls were waiting for my ass. I made it to Angie house within fifteen minutes. I noticed Mel and Money's cars and thought to myself I should just keep going, but I had to face Mel, and today was just as good as any. I knocked on the door, and RJ opened it.

"Hey, Nel," he said, and I walked in.

I spoke to everyone and made my way upstairs. I was practically running. I didn't want Mel to stop me.

"Look who decided to join us, little miss whore," Angie teased.

"OMG, you guys, really? I was going to tell you, but—"

I stopped talking and closed the door. I didn't want Mel to hear me.

"Okay, so yesterday after I finish my paper, it was about 9:00 pm. I was hungry but didn't have anything to eat, so I went to Wal-Mart. I'm shopping and the last thing I needed was bottled waters. It was too high up and out of nowhere, Real comes and gets them down for me. He talked about how he told Sha to have me call him, and I told him I lost his number."

I noticed I was still standing, so I sat down and finished.

"So, he said to call him so that he knew I made it home. I was so worn out that when I hit the bed, I was knocked out." I looked to see if they were following me.

"Okay, go on. I know it's more," Sha said.

"Well, like I said, I fell asleep. So, peep game, this nigga calls me, and I didn't give him my number, so I thought maybe you did, Sha," I looked at Sha.

"No! I didn't give it to him," Sha laughed.

"Well, come to find out, this nigga somehow got my phone at the club that night and called his phone from mine. That nigga slick," I smiled just thinking about him.

"So, how was the date?" Angie asked.

"It was just lunch, and we're just friends, but he is so sweet. I like him as a friend though," I responded trying to hide my smile Real put on my face.

Sha and Angie looked at each other.

"Why y'all looking like that? That's all that happened. We hugged in a friendly way, though."

"Yeah, okay, Nel. You lying, though. You like him. I can see it on your face," Angie confessed.

"Girl, whatever. Y'all crazy. I do not like him like that. I mean, he's cool, but I just got out of a relationship if you two haven't forgotten," I said as I reclined on Angie's bed.

"Why y'all asses didn't tell me he was here? Y'all know I don't want to see him. He just makes me want to shoot him every time I see him," I said, referring to Mel.

We talked a little more before we went downstairs to the guys. We wanted to know about this bachelor's party.

The guys were just getting up when we came downstairs. The guys walked outside, and we followed.

"So, what's up with this bachelor's party?" Angie asked, looking at Mel and Money.

"Why you looking at me? Y'all know what's gon' be there—naked bitches and liquor. Now, if you want to know if RJ's ass gon' behave himself, hell yeah! I'll make sure of that," Money joked.

"Okay, I'm holding you to that," Angie joked.

"That's why y'all asses followed us out here to ask us about that shit? Y'all crazy," RJ said as he put his arm around Angie and leaned against my car.

"Well, I came because I want y'all to beat Benz ass for me when y'all see him. That nigga been talking shit on the phone," Sha said, causing everyone to laugh. We all knew how Benz was.

I felt like an outcast now. I just leaned against the back of Angie's car and looked at my friends all chatting together.

"Baby, what you get me to wear to the wedding?" RJ asked.

"Um, come see real quick. It's nice, though," Angie said.

"Shit, let me see too because I have no damn clue what to wear to a wedding. Shit, I'll come in that bitch fresh with some True Religion shit on," Money laughed.

They walked in the house leaving Mel, Sha, and I outside.

"Yeah, okay?" was all I heard Sha say before she walked off, I'm guessing Mel gave a signal for her to leave.

When Sha took off, I was walking behind her. I didn't want to be alone with him.

"Hey, Chanel. Can I holler at you real quick?" Mel asked.

This was the first time in a while hearing Mel call out my whole name. I stopped. I didn't want to, but did. I sat on the step looking at him. How I could be so stupid? All the signs were there; he came and left when he pleased. He came home late, using the hustle as an excuse. I knew in the back of my mind he could've been cheating, but I never would have believed it.

"Nel, I'm leaving tomorrow morning, and I hope when I get back, we can settle this and move on whether it's with or without me. I don't want any bad feelings between us. I would like to be friends if you don't want to work things out between us. My mom called, and I told her what happened. She was upset, but she said she understood why you left," Mel said as he sat next to me.

"Do you understand why I left, Mel?" I asked, looking directly into his eyes.

"Yes, I do now after she explained it to me, but I just don't want us beefing when we hang with the same crew. We can be cordial to one another; don't you think?" Mel asked, looking at me.

"Yes, it wouldn't be so awkward then," I answered back.

"Nel, I love you so much. If you give me a second chance, I promise I'll do right by you."

"Mel, I can't, and I don't want to talk about this now. It's too emotional for me," I said.

"I'm sorry, baby, I just need you in my life. I know when I get back we can try to at least give it a try," he said.

"Mel, at this point. I can't say yes or no because I am beyond hurt. I'm trying to hide it, but you can't think I'm okay with it. Let's just drop it for now," I said.

"Well, I guess I got to deal with Benz's ass tomorrow. I already know he's waiting on me," Mel joked.

"I don't think he waiting for that reason. He knows that I wouldn't want him to hurt you even if we're not together," I confessed.

"So, I guess that's it. I mean, I'm gon' be real with you. I'm still gon' try and fix this, but I will respect your wishes," Mel hugged me. We heard someone laugh behind us. So, we turned around.

"Y'all so nosey!" Mel said as he stood up.

"So, y'all back together now?" Money asked, and it seemed as if everyone else waited for a response.

"No, we're just trying to dead the beef between us and make things easier. We good, though. I'm giving my baby some space. She ain't trying to replace a nigga," Mel joked and pushed me a little.

Mel always tried to show off in front of his boys.

"Y'all wack," Money laughed.

"Well, I'm heading home, guys. I'm tired," I said.

"When your ass going back to work?" Money joked.

"Why, nigga? I ain't broke," I said as I pretended to fight him. "But I took another week off. Too much shit been going on."

"Well, see y'all later," Money got into his car pulled off.

Sha and Mel left next and then me. I was still hurt about Mel cheating, but I was taking it better than most women could have.

I went home, made me some tea, and sat down next to my computer. My teacher hadn't graded my paper yet, so I logged off. I started thinking about Real. *What if we did have potential to have a relationship? Where would that leave Mel? Would he be hurt? Would he move on?* It hurt me to think of Mel with someone else, but I remembered he already had been, and ain't no telling how many others. I already made my appointment with Sonto, and I knew she had all the latest gossip. I couldn't wait until tomorrow morning.

Nel

$\mathcal{I}$t was 7:30 am when I rolled out of bed. My hair appointment was at 9:00 am, and if I was even one minute late, Sonto would have someone else in the chair. I ate a bagel before I showered.

I dressed in a grey blouse with blue and grey skinny jeans. I called Sha and told her I was going to the Salon and if I was in there past three o'clock to go and find me an outfit for the barbecue. Fridays were Sonto's busiest days, and he usually started at eight o'clock sharp. I made up my bed and walked downstairs. I grabbed my charger to my phone and left out the door.

Mel texted me and said they were about to hit the highway and asked if he could meet up to get a quick hug, I told him yeah, and he was already outside of my condo. I don't know why I said that, but I did. My feelings were all over the place.

"Hey, Mel. I'm in a rush, so I can't talk long," I walked up to him.

"I just came for a hug. You never know, Benz might kill me other there," he joked, and I laughed and hugged him back.

Mel looked at me while hugging me and asked for a kiss.

"Mel, please don't do this."

"Nel, I'm sorry I hurt you, but I still love you. I miss making love to you at night. I miss you making me breakfast followed by more sex. I miss us, Nel. Just think about all you will be giving up on us, we have too much history," Mel said as he held me close.

"Mel I miss us too, but you have to understand I need my space you showing up here asking for a hug is bad enough, now you telling me all this," I said, feeling confused about my feelings.

"Nel, I know what I did was wrong and stupid, but people make mistakes. You're right, I need to give you your space, but it's hard watching the one you love slip away." He looked into my eyes.

I remember when it felt good being in his arms, but now it felt like it was just because he was telling me all the right things.

"I know you want space and after today, I swear I will back off, but please just one last kiss, Nel, please," he begged.

I hated to see him beg, but he deserved to be out there begging for me to come back. I've been begging for his time for years now, and now that it seems like I got it, I don't know if it's what I really want anymore. I gave in just so he could leave. We kissed like we were a couple in love, but it felt different to me. It felt like the love wasn't there, and I knew right then and there it was really over. As soon as Mel got it, we both would be better off.

I pulled my car out of the garage and made my way to the salon. I didn't regret the kiss between us because it was a goodbye kiss for me. Mel said fuck my feelings when he cheated, so fuck his!

Mel

$\mathcal{I}$ really wanted things to work out between Nel and I. I loved her more than anything. Yes, I fucked other bitches from time to time, but if she would give me a second chance I would gladly ease up. I couldn't say I'd stop completely because I'd be lying. I would try harder, but I needed for her to confirm that we were back together before I dropped all my hoes.

The kiss between us felt different. It felt like she wasn't really into the kiss. I know that I fucked up major this time around. I'm not really confident that she would come back to me, but I'd be damned if she goes off and be with another nigga. That shit wasn't happening. I needed to clear my head from the shit, because it was stressing me out. I was excited to be getting away for a hot second. I needed a little time away, and the bachelor party is exactly what I needed. I know Benz would have a whole lecture coming my way but shit, his ass did Sha the same way, even worse if you ask me.

I stopped back by my house to make sure my shit was locked up. I waited on the crew so we could hit the highway. We were all riding in one car, probably Money's since he had the truck. My phone vibrated, and it was Candy. Her ass was really starting to get on my nerves. She heard around that Nel and I broke up, and she constantly called me. I didn't feel like being bothered with her, so I thumbed her ass.

Nel

I made it to the salon just in time, Sonto washed and conditioned my hair. I was chatting and laughing when my phone rang.

"Hello?" I laughed into the phone.

"What up, C. What you doing this morning beautiful?" Real asked.

"Oh, just getting my hair done for wedding. Remember the one I told you about?" I smiled.

"Oh yeah, I forgot. Okay, I just wanted to hear your voice and see what was up."

"Okay, talk to you later," I said, hanging up.

I texted Sha, and she said she had just finished getting her house in order for her son. He would be back home in a few days, and she didn't want to spend the weekend preparing for her baby boy. She had to remove all the stuff she left lying around like knives, scissors, pencils, or anything that could possibly hurt him. Not too long after, she texted saying she was on her way to the salon.

"Chanel, you got all this damn hair and always putting weave in it," Sonto said as he worked his magic.

"So, I like weave, boo. Who gon' check me!" I laughed. "So, Sonto, fill your girl in. I know you heard about me and Mel's break-up, so what the streets talking about?

"Man, I didn't want to bring it up because I didn't know if you were cool with it, but bitch, niggas talking about he cheated with some bitch named Kim. Peep this, he's been fucking with this bitch name Candy, and that's not all. He's been fucking her for almost a year now. Candy was in here a month ago, bragging about Mel giving her money to get her hair done and bitch, you know me. I'm like shit, Chanel can buy her own damn hair and pay to get it done, and she can go out and buy an outfit and a car that match. That bitch was looking so stupid. Her ass was quiet from then on out," Sonto said.

I wasn't hurt. I was pissed. I wanted to call and curse Mel's ass out. I remained calm and got all the information I needed. I wasn't really tripping off Sonto not telling me she wasn't the type to bring drama to anyone unless you asked her for information, and I respected that.

"Where those bitches be at?" I asked because I knew a lot of females but didn't fuck with them.

"Candy lives in them raggedy ass apartment's downtown and Kim, girl I don't know, but I got a picture of her in my phone because I did her this bad ass style!" Sonto showed me the picture of Kim.

"Oh, okay. She cute, but she ain't me!" I laughed

"Okay, bitch!" Sonto said as she gave me a high five.

I was about to ask another question when Sha walked in the salon.

"Oh hell, two bad bitches at the same damn time!" Sonto yelled out and ran to hug Sha.

"Hey, boo. Long time, bitch!" Sha laughed.

"Shit, y'all bitches need to be working in here. Y'all the ones who be doing hair and shit!" Sonto said.

"Why? So, I can kill a bitch? I'm straight. Besides, I only do my hair because you always overbooking motherfuckers!" Sha laughed.

"Sonto, tell her what you told me about Mel because I'm still trying to digest the shit!" I told her.

Sonto went on to tell Sha what she had previously told me before Sha walked in as she finished up my hair.

"Are you fucking kidding me? That bitch ass nigga!" Sha said pissed.

Sha was pissed, but she knew I had this let no nigga see you sweat policy. We chatted a little bit more before Sha and I left. We called Angie and told her to meet us at the mall. I dropped my car off at home and rode with Sha.

"Okay, Nel, tell me what's up. How you feel about this shit?"

"First off, this nigga came to my crib this morning asking for a hug and he talked some slick shit about how he misses me. You know I'm not buying the shit, though. So, the whole time this nigga holding onto me and kissing all on me!"

"Bitch you kissed him that's why his ass thinks he still got you! Sha said as she turned into the mall parking lot.

"Bitch, I gave him a kiss because shit, I'm like this a goodbye kiss for me. I'm done with his ass. Then Sonto lay this shit on me. I just feel like man, I played the fool for too long, but now that we're broken up,

I'm not as pissed as I should be. This just gives me more courage to leave and move on."

"That's what I like to hear. We're some strong bitches over here. Fuck a weak bitch!" Sha said, and I laughed.

Angie was closer to the mall, so she was already there waiting inside by the door.

"Hey, ladies," Angie greeted us.

"Bitch, why you look sad?" Sha asked Angie.

"Because my man just left for three days, and I'm gon' be all alone," Angie said and then laughed.

We knew she would miss him, but she would be okay. We walked into the mall and did a little shopping. Victoria's Secret had sale that we couldn't pass up on. We got sexy panties, bras, and lingerie. I felt that I didn't have anybody to wear it for. We sat by the food court, ate and talked, and of course I gave Angie the rundown about what Sonto told me.

Angie was pissed, but she knew I could handle the situation. We decided to get dressed at my house for the barbecue. El's house was closest to mine. It was Friday, so of course, we had wine on deck. We had a lil' pre-turn-up before the barbecue.

"Real's ass gon' be surprised when he see you," Sha yelled as she walked from the kitchen.

"I know, but shit, I figure if he thinks I'm not coming, he'll have his other boo there. That way I can see how real Leon really is!" I said.

"Is that his real name?" Angie asked.

"Yes, it is!" I smiled.

"What the fuck you smiling at? Let me find out!" Angie teased.

"Bitch, bye! Find out what?" I laughed.

We dropped the subject and got dressed. It was now 7:45 pm, and El said for us to come by about 8:00 pm. I had two bathrooms and two bedrooms in my condo, so it didn't take us long to get ready.

I was dressed first in a grey and pink romper that had my ass looking good enough to eat. I had on some grey heels. I made sure to grab my silver MK sandals that matched my MK watch.

Sha was next to finish getting dressed. She wore a peach, sleeveless blouse with tan and peach leggings that had a peach line going down the sides. She had on some gold and peach sandals with gold accessories. Angie was last as always. She wore a black and cream halter top with black, ripped, skinny jeans. She had some cream sandals with gold accessories.

"We look so hot!" I said as I looked in the mirror.

"Hell yeah!" Angie said as she sipped her wine.

We finished our glasses of wine and made our way over to El's house. When we got there, the block was packed that we had to park five houses down. It was so many expensive cars people couldn't help but notice these niggas were paid, but that didn't impress us. We had our own. Sha walked into the backyard first to find El; he was by the barbecue grilled turning the ribs over.

"Hey, sexy. Glad you could make it. Where your crew at?" El asked as he hugged her.

"They're by the fence where Real at. You want to surprise him now or what?"

"Oh yeah, I forgot Nel is his surprise. Let me go get him," El said, walking off.

Angie walked in she said she wasn't there for Real, so she felt like she should already be inside. El came back with Real, and Real hugged Sha and Angie. I could see him from the slight slit in the wooden fence.

"Aye, man, I got a surprise for you, but you got to close your eyes for this one, bro," El said as he smiled.

Real closed his eyes, and Angie came and got me. When El told Real to open his eyes, I was right in front of him.

"Damn, sexy, I just knew they had some corny ass shit going on," Real hugged me.

Damn, this nigga smells so good. I thought to myself.

"This the best gift I got all day," Real said as he licked his lips.

"Y'all come on back so we can get the party started," El said as he led us to the back.

The scenery was nice. El sat us at an empty table. El and Real excused themselves so they could say hi to some guests.

"This is nice," Angie said.

"It sure is. Did you see how Real's eyes lit up when he saw Nel?" Sha mentioned.

"Yeah, let me find out y'all got something going on you're not telling us about," Angie joked.

"Y'all so crazy. We're just friends!" I said.

146

"I wish you would stop with the just friend shit. You know you want him and from his eyes, he wants you too and after that shit with Mel, you better grab Real's ass up," Sha said, laughing but being serious.

"OMG! Okay, yes, I'm feeling him, but I got to work on myself first. How does that make me look getting out of one relationship and jumping into another?" I said.

"No, you don't have shit that needs work. Mel's ass fucked up, not you, and you know my motto, one nigga fucks up and let the next nigga luck up!" Sha said.

"I know, but I'm still healing. That'll make Real like my rebound, and I don't want to seem like I'm using him," I said.

"Nel, on the real, Mel was your first, so I can understand that, but you deserve to be happy, so just let go tonight, be free and live," Angie said to me.

A few fellows made their way over trying to holler, that's when I noticed Real and El making their way back over.

"Yo', El, this you?" the guy asked, seeing that El was smiling at Sha.

"Yes, sir," El answered back.

"That's all me, Aaron," Real said to his homeboy, who was damn near drooling over me.

Once the other fellows left, we started to relax and just have fun.

"Aye, y'all want a drink?" the men asked.

"Sure, what y'all got?" all three of us said at once.

"Y'all triplets or something?" El laughed, walking us over to the bar.

We decided on Ciroc and Cranberry juice. Angie spoke to Saun when he came over to speak to us.

"Hey, ladies. Y'all the coldest female out here tonight," he said.

Saun walked over to Angie and stared her up and down.

Everyone busted out laughing because homeboy didn't care. He was checking Angie's ass out.

"We'll nice seeing you too, Saun!" Angie said.

"Oh, you remember my name, so I must've been on your mind?"

"Um, no, but I never forget a handsome face," Angie laughed at him.

"So, how you been, sexy? Your man taking good care of you? If not, Saun here can very well do that!" We all laughed and headed back over to our table.

Everyone was having a good time. Real was all up on me, and I didn't mind it one bit. El was sitting at the bar with Sha, laughing at some guy doing the Dougie. Dude needed to sit his corny ass down.

Real's mother came out the house with the cake, and Real wanted to introduce me to her, but I thought it may be too soon. Everyone sang happy birthday. I couldn't help but notice how beautiful Real's mother was, and he looked just like her. I also noticed some female mugging me throughout the party and was rolling her eyes and everything. I wanted to ask the bitch did she have a problem. I thought maybe it was Real's lil' chick or something, but the way he was hugged up with me, you wouldn't think so.

Real blew out his candles and hugged his mom. Real's mom cut everybody a slice of cake. After she got done, she pulled Real to the side. I was watching her throughout the party because she glanced at me and smiled like she knew something I didn't. Real called me over to him and his mom. I was nervous as fuck. I could kick his ass. I knew this would happen because he kept looking over at me.

"Hello!" I said right away to the beautiful woman in front of me.

"Mom, this is Chanel. Chanel, this is my mother, Sandy Ross, but you can call her Ms. Ross," Real said.

"Nice to meet you, baby," she said.

"Likewise!" I said.

"So, baby, how long have you and Leon been dating?" she asked me.

I was shocked. I wasn't expecting that. I looked at Real for help, but when he didn't, I said, "I…um…we're just friends, Ms. Ross!"

"Oh, I'm just teasing, baby. I know you two are good friends." I smiled, knowing that Ms. Ross was just playing because I thought I was about to faint.

We talked for a good hour before Ms. Ross said she was leaving for the night. She asked that I come over and hang with her sometime. Of course, I agreed because she was a wise woman. Ms. Ross told Real to walk her to her car so she could talk to him.

Real

"Baby, I like her. She's smart and graduating soon, no kids, and she works. You better be trying to make her your wife boy!" my mom joked.

"Okay, mom. I'll work on that tonight, I promise," I laughed.

"I bet you will, baby," she smiled.

My mom left, and I headed toward the back when Meka walked up to me and said. "Who is that bitch you're all over and you letting your mom meet?"

"Hold the fuck up. We ain't together in case you forgot. You better gon' on with that shit, Meka!" I said. I was pissed that this thirsty bitch would approach me like she ain't fucking every nigga in the party.

"Oh, so it's like that? The other night you couldn't keep your dick out my mouth!"

"Look, Meka, I'm not your man. I let you suck my shit and that was all, and that was the last time, so push on for you piss me off!" I said with so much base in my voice that she was already walking off, but not before she turned around to make one last remark.

"That's why Saun and El's dick bigger than your shit anyway."

I couldn't help but laugh, because in the past, my boys and I ran the bust down on the bitch. El and Saun wanted to go before me because her shit would be open to wide after I got done. I knew I had to stop fucking with her ass. She was just too thirsty for me.

I walked back over to Nel and her girls when I overheard them talking.

"You want to beat that bitch down. Just say the word!" Angie said.

"Naw, she ain't worth my time or buzz," I laughed.

"So, you got your lil' boo rolling her eyes at me. What's up with that?" She asked.

"Shit, Nel, on the real tip, I don't know. I mean, I fucked and let her suck my dick a few times, that's it, but shit, every nigga in here did."

"Okay!" was all she said.

"So, what? Is it a problem or something? I told you she ain't my girl or side piece; she ain't nothing to me for real." I asked.

"I feel like you're telling the truth, but I can't put shit pass niggas these days. I'm good, though. I just asked. I don't want to ruin your birthday, so let's drop it. We're just friends anyway. I just wanted to know why she would be mugging me and I don't even know her!"

"Man, fuck her, but you made my birthday special coming here to celebrate with me, talking about you going to a wedding, but really trying to surprise a nigga and shit," I whispered in her ear.

"So, do I get my gift now or later?" I whispered in her ear again.

"I thought I was your gift," she whispered back.

"Well, when can I open my gift?" I licked her ear. I noticed Nel squeezing her legs together.

"You so nasty!" she said, smiling.

Somebody had turned the music all the way up and niggas was dancing up on every ass that was shaking.

I asked Nel did she want to dance.

"No, I don't dance anymore," she laughed.

"Shit, when did you stop because you had a nigga dick hard as fuck at the club!" we both smiled.

Nel

*I*t was getting toward the end of the party, and everyone told Real happy birthday while walking toward the front. Angie was sitting on Saun's lap when Sha looked over at them.

"Nel, check Angie out. You know she drunk," Sha said.

I looked over in Angie's direction and laughed.

"Yeah, I better get her home," I shook my head.

Real was walking back over to me when Meka walked up and said, "Happy birthday. If you want your gift, call me."

"Oh, that won't be happening. My girl got something for me already," Real said as he sat next to me.

I guess Meka felt stupid because she just walked off looking crazy. I shook my head.

Thirsty bitch! I thought to myself.

"Well, we better get going too. It's 2:30 am," I said as I stood up and walked toward Angie.

"Hey, Angie, we about to go."

"Okay, I'm ready, bye Saun," she said."

"Bye, sexy, wish you didn't have to go home to your man," Saun said going into the house.

Angie and I burst out and laughing as we walked toward Real, El, and Sha.

"Hey, ladies, Sha gon' hang back with me. Is that okay?" El asked.

"She grown, boo!" I said.

"You don't want to hang longer? Come on, the night still young!" Real grabbed me by the waist.

"No, I better go. I'm tired anyway, and Angie's ass is drunk."

Angie couldn't even say anything to defend herself. She was barely able to stand straight.

"Okay. Well, I'll walk you ladies to the car," Real said.

He walked us to the car, helped Angie get in, and hugged me once again. He said he really didn't want me to go, and I didn't want to, but I needed to because I couldn't control the feelings I had around him.

"Bye, C!" he said.

"Bye, Leon," I said back.

"Call me when you get home, okay?"

"Okay. I will this time. I promise," I laughed.

I drove home in silence. I couldn't help but think of Real. He was funny, sexy, and played close attention to me. If I move a hand, he would follow it. After we made it home safe, I got Angie in the house and into the guest bedroom. I showered and called Real to let him know we made it home okay. I fell asleep and two hours went by when my cell phone rang.

"Hello?"

It was Mel calling, and I thought something could be wrong since he was calling at 4:00 am.

"Hello!"

I said louder, hearing loud music in his background. I was about to hang up when I heard him moaning.

"Oh yeah, bitch. Ride this dick, baby. Oh yeah, just like that, baby!"

I couldn't believe this shit. Mel must've called me on accident, and I was pissed he was fucking God knows who. I was stuck listening to my ex fucking on my phone. Finally, I had enough and hung up. I don't know why, but I just cried myself to sleep.

Sha

*E*l was getting me so turned on he kissed all over my body, he grabbed my ass, and tried to unbutton my blouse. I knew we were at Real's house, so I stopped him.

"El, can you take me back to Nel's house, please? It's late, and I should go."

"I really want you to stay, but if you really want to leave then okay." He kissed me.

On the ride to Nel's house, El talked about how much he wanted to fuck me. I was getting hot. I needed to get away from him. We made it to Nel's house, and he walked me to the door.

"Shit, I forgot my key inside, and my phone dead!" I said.

I rang the doorbell six times before Nel came to the door.

"Nel, I'm so sorry I left my key. Wait, were you crying? Nel, what's wrong?"

"Why this nigga called me on accident and had the nerve to be fucking in the background?" Nel said with tears in her eyes.

"Nel, fuck him. It's over so you got to accept the fact that he gon' continue to do him.

"I'm so sorry, El. You probably think all I do is cry?" Nel said. I guess she finally noticed him.

"No, I know that's not true because my boy had you smiling and blushing. Yeah, I peeped game," El joked. Nel agreed and went back to her room.

"Can I chill for a bit? I just want to at least taste it?" El asked as he rubbed my pussy through my pants.

"Boy, this is not my house, and Nel wouldn't approve you chilling over here!"

"Nel won't approve of who chilling over here?" she said coming, back into the room with her robe on.

"This is my house. He can chill. Y'all can go in the basement and watch TV," she said.

Nel had her whole basement furnished with a nice sofa and a flat screen TV.

"Okay. We'll be quiet!" El said as we headed for the basement.

"Well, in that case, make sure y'all put a towel down and turn some music on down there, love birds," Nel yelled out.

I was walking off when I heard El talking to Real on the phone.

"Aye, man, you need to call your girl. Ol' boy done fucked up and butt dialed her, and she heard that nigga fucking on the phone!" I heard El say.

I couldn't hear what Real said, but I was sure he probably was going to hit Nel up.

Real

"Hello!" Nel said into the phone, sounding sad.

"Dang, did I call at a bad time?" I asked her.

"No, you're straight, Real."

"What's wrong? Why you sound so sad?"

"I…um…I don't," she said.

"Nel, don't lie to me. I hate that!"

"I…um…I overheard Mel fucking on my phone. He called me on accident."

"Damn, C!"

"Yeah, I'm good. I guess I just feel some type of way. You know your boy over here?" she asked.

"Who, El?" I asked, already knowing.

"Yea, El. Who else?" She laughed.

"Oh, okay. That's what up."

She sighed into the phone.

"I wish I could take your pain away and make you happy. I just want to hug you and tell you it's gon' be alright, C."

"I want you to hug me too!" she confessed.

I couldn't believe she said that. "Oh, you do?"

"Yes, I do, Leon." It was quiet for a brief second. "Can you come through? I know it's late, and you probably had other plans."

"Yeah, I can do that. Are you sure?" I asked.

"Yes, I'm sure," she said.

"Well, what's your address? I would love to come spend more time with you and hug you," I said.

She told me her address. When I pulled up, I thought I was tripping. Now, I knew this was the house I seen Mel at, hugging some chick. Now, it made more sense why she was so heartbroken; they had gotten back together. I called her to let her know I was outside. When she opened the door, I gave her as evil look.

"Why you looking at me like that?" She asked.

I shut the door, took off my shoes, and followed her up to her room.

"Nel, I got to ask you something, and please keep it real with me!"

"Okay, what is it?" she asked.

"Yesterday, when I rode pass here, I seen Mel hugging a female outside of this house, but I couldn't see who that female was…was that you?"

"You stay in the Paradise Condo's?" she asked not even answering the question.

"Yes, but please, answer my question!"

"Yes, Real, it was me, but it wasn't what you think. It's complicated, but we're no longer together."

I just looked at her. "What the fuck is complicated? Either you're together or not," I said.

"We're not together. It's complicated in ways I can't explain, but it is over between us. Do you believe me?" she asked so soft and innocently that I just wanted to fuck her pain away.

"Why were you crying when you heard him fucking on the phone?"

"I really don't know, Real. I'm just so overwhelmed with everything, but I swear I hugged and kissed him goodbye one last time because I'm done with him!"

"Does he know that?" I asked.

"Yes. I mean…I don't…I assume…he should," she said.

"Okay, if you say it's over, I believe you, Chanel."

She walked over to me and stared into my eyes. I wanted to kiss her and from the look on her face, she wanted me to.

"I thought you came to hug me?" she said.

Her robe was open, and I thought she looked so sexy in boy shorts and wife beater. I wanted to do more than hug, but I had to respect her. I knew she was vulnerable.

"I did," I said as I watched her get in her bed under her covers.

I took that as my cue to get in with her. I wrapped my arms around her waist as I lied slightly between her legs.

"You're so sweet. You really are a good friend," she said.

I couldn't take it. I had to kiss her. My tongue tangled with hers, and we shared a passionate kiss for what seem like an hour. I slid my hand around to her ass, and I started rubbing on her.

I kissed her neck and pulled up her wife beater and sucked her nipples. She started moaning. I pulled her boy shorts off and kissed her belly and made my way down. I was kissing and licking down by her pelvis and she started dripping. I kissed her inner thigh and finally kissed her pretty pussy. I guess she liked that shit because she was already cumming. I knew then she wasn't going to be able to handle the dick. I got up and removed my pants.

"Are you sure you want this? If you're not ready, then I understand," I asked.

"Yes, I'm sure," she answered.

That's all the confirmation I needed. I pulled my boxers off and grabbed a condom out of my wallet and slid it on. Nel was too busy looking at my twelve inches that she didn't notice me smiling at her.

"You okay, baby?" I asked.

"Um, yes, I'm good."

I slid in bed on top of her, I gently put the head of my penis inside of her. She was too damn tight. I know for a fact Mel wasn't hitting her shit right.

"Damn, Nel, you so tight, baby. I don't want to hurt you."

"It's okay. I can take it," She whispered in my ear.

I finally got in her pussy. It felt so good, I wanted to take that damn condom off.

"You feel so good, C. I like how your pussy wraps around my dick!"

She didn't respond with words but more of a moan.

"Oh, baby, please don't stop!" she said as she noticed I slowed down.

I started going faster since she wanted it so bad. I put her legs over my shoulders and started deep stroking her, giving her my signature dick. I had to admit her shit was so good. After her cumming again, I came after her, and I finally gave her a break.

"Damn, C, that shit felt so good." She was just staring at me. I hoped she wasn't regretting it. "You okay?" I asked.

"Yes, I'm great now," she said as she bit the bottom of her lip.

"Good, but I thought you just wanted a hug?" I said as I laid closer to her.

"I did, but you can't keep them hands to yourself, and your touch does something to me."

"Oh really? So, what are we, best friends now?" I joked, caressing her face with my hand.

"I guess!" she said.

"I want you to be my girl."

She was quiet. I hated when she did that. It meant she was over thinking shit.

"I don't know what to say," she finally said.

"You don't have to say anything. Just think about it, talk about it with your girls or whatever you got to do?"

"Okay. Are you still taking me to the movies tomorrow?" she asked.

"Oh, I forgot about that. I shouldn't since you lied about going to a wedding."

"Oh, you mad at me after I gave you birthday sex?" she smiled.

"Yes, baby, we can do that, and thanks for the birthday sex. I better get home. It is way past your bedtime, Ms. Chanel," I laughed.

"Oh, shut up!" She tried pushing me out the bed.

We made it down stairs, and El and Sha was on the couch smiling.

"Well, well, well, look who's here, Super Save a Hoe," Sha and El laughed.

"Oh, y'all funny, huh?" I said as I turned around to hug Nel before I left.

El got up, hugged Sha, and left with me.

El's nosey ass came back to my house to get the information on what went down. He didn't expect to see me at Nel's house. We got in the house, and the questions began.

"Man, what the hell were you doing at Chanel's house, nigga?"

"Shit, man, she was a little bothered by that shit with ol' boy. I'm like I wish I could hug you and shit. Next thing I know, she asked me to come over!"

"Okay, so what you hugged her? Nigga, I know you. You tried something, didn't you?"

"Fuck you, nigga, you don't know me, but shit I started rubbing on her soft ass. One thing led to another and next thing I know I'm fucking the shit out of her. Man, she had the tightest, wettest pussy ever, man. I think I'm in love!"

"Nigga, let me find out you ain't joking, but shit I'm digging Sha too. She's so soft like I like them." El rubbed his hands together.

We kicked it and talked a little while longer. El slept in one of my guest rooms, and I headed up to my room, showered, and dozed off.

Angie

RJ called me twice, and I was just now calling back. It was 9:30 am. I usually always answered for him even if I was in a meeting at work. So, I know he's probably worried.

"Hey, bae, I was sleep when you called last night. What's good?" I said into the phone.

"What's good? Angie, you always answer your phone for me. What was y'all doing at the club last night?"

"Nothing. We were just chilling and drinking… nothing major, but I had one too many, so we all stayed over Nel's house."

"Oh ok, your ass need to calm that drinking down, woman!" RJ laughed.

"I miss you, baby," I told him.

"I miss you too, girl. Well, go get yourself together and call me later. I got to get ready for this wedding. I can't believe I'm going to a wedding without my girl!" RJ laughed.

"Shit, me either. Maybe you will get some ideas!" I joked.

"Okay, girl. Talk to you later." His ass was rushing me off the phone now.

"Bye, baby," We hung up, and I went to join the ladies in the kitchen.

"So y'all bitches cooking breakfast in shit. Them niggas got y'all asses right I see!" I said as I teased my sisters. Nel woke me up early in the morning to tell me about what happened between her and Real. I was happy for her.

"Shit, Real sure did, and why your drunk ass was all over Saun? What's up with that?" Nel asked, looking at me.

"I was just chilling. He cool. I like him!"

"Nope. We better than that, and we don't hold true feelings from each other. So, Angie, what's really going on?" Sha asked, fixing my plate.

"Man, I really don't know. He just pays attention to the little things that RJ takes for granted. Our relationship is becoming boring and that scares me," I confessed to the girls.

"Damn, really? I mean, you can't just cheat on him and think everything gon' be alright. Damn, Angie! RJ really loves you. He's one of the good ones," Nel said, eating her food.

"I'm not going to cheat on him. I know it's probably just a phase I'm going through. There's nothing to worry about, ladies!"

We left the conversation at that and talked about what our plans were for the day. Nel was going to the movies with Real later at and wanted to double date with Sha and El, but I didn't want to be alone.

"I guess I can catch up on so work while y'all bitches out," I laughed, getting ready to head home.

"Okay, Nel, I'm leaving. See you later at the movies!" Sha said, walking out the door.

Nel

I fell back to sleep for a few hours before I cleaned my house and bathed. The doorbell rang, and I thought it was Sha coming back over, but when I opened the door, it was a man holding flowers.

"Hello, I'm looking for a Chanel," the delivery guy said.

"Yes, I'm Chanel!" He gave the flowers to me, and I read the card that was attached.

It read *"You're something special. I hope you're still thinking!"*

I knew exactly who sent them. Real wanted me to be his girl.

OMG! How can you like someone so much in such short time? I thought to myself. I called him to thank him.

"Hey, beautiful," he answered right away.

"Leon, you're so sweet. Thank you for the flowers. They are so beautiful."

"You deserve them," he said.

"I can't wait to see you later. I've been thinking about you all day," he confessed.

I was speechless. I didn't know how to feel. I thought it was too good to be true. If I took things further, would he eventually change?

"You're so sweet, Real. Thank you!" I told him.

"Stop saying that. You deserve to be treated like a queen every day and if you give me a chance, you would be!"

I sat on the phone. He was saying all the right things, but how could I trust him so easily after what Mel did to me.

"Okay. Well, Sha and I will meet you guys at the movies."

"Oh yeah, my boy wanted to take Angie to the movies just as friends, though, you know?" I laughed and said I would ask Angie and call him back.

I waited until Angie answered her phone.

"Hey, Angie, Saun wanted to know if you would go to the movies with him."

"Nel, y'all so funny. Stop playing!"

"Bitch, I'm for real. Real just called and asked that way you don't have to sit home and work all Saturday."

"I guess. Let me get myself ready. Who's driving?" she asked, sounding excited.

"You can come over here, and y'all can ride with me, or Sha can drive. It don't matter."

"Okay, I'll be over in a little while!" We ended our call.

Angie and Sha finally made it to my house. We got in my car to head to the movies, the guys were there waiting on us as soon as we got there. When we got out, the guys greeted us. Saun took it further by kissing Angie on the cheek. Real opened the door for me, but a couple was walking out, so I waited until they got out the door, but the guy stopped and stared a hole in Real's head.

"You got a problem with your fucking eyes, nigga?" Real asked like he was ready for war.

The guy just kept going and didn't say shit. Saun's ass was ready to fuck him up, but Angie told him to just calm down. The guys bought the tickets while we got the popcorn and snacks. We all sat in the same row with a few seats in between us.

When the previews went off, Real leaned over and snuck a kiss from me. I just smiled because I really liked it. He pulled me close. and we watched the movie. I looked over and saw Saun was rubbing Angie's leg across his lap. She was acting like it was just natural. I made a mental note to talk to her later about that shit. El was holding on to Sha while watching the movie. Everyone seemed to be having a good time.

Mel

The guys and I were just getting back from the wedding. We wanted to change for the reception. I got a call from my boy.

"Aye, nigga, tell them they got to hold off until I touch down!" I said into the phone.

"Nigga, that's not why I'm calling. I'm calling because I just seen your bitch with that nigga, Real, going into the movies and check game, her girl, Sha, was with her too. I didn't see who the other niggas were. I was too busy mugging that nigga, Real!" my homeboy told me.

"Man, what the fuck?" I knew my nigga had no reason to lie. "Good looking, man. I'll get at you."

I walked into in the living room of the hotel and told Benz what was going on. The shit with Nel was my problem, but I knew he would've jumped on the shit about Sha. We called the girl's' phone back to back, and none of them answered, not even Angie. RJ was now pissed; he thought his girl was cheating on him. He tried calling again but still no answer.

"Man, I'm gon' kill that nigga. That's the same nigga in the club that was all over Nel!" I was on fire.

"Man, fuck this we can go pack our shit. I'll hit my homeboy up, and we can fly over there and be there in like an hour!" Benz said pissed off.

Benz wanted to catch Sha as up so bad. My homie was crazy like that for real.

"Shit, I'm ready!" RJ said. Money and Cruz just looked around. They didn't care either way. They had their fun last night anyway.

Nel

$\mathcal{I}$ looked at my phone, and it was Mel. I saw Angie and Sha looking at their phones also. We looked at each other, and the guys started looking at us like something was up. I told Real I was going to the bathroom, and Sha and Angie followed.

"Man, these niggas keep calling. You think something could be wrong?" Sha asked.

"Let me call RJ and see. Hold on." Angie called RJ on speaker.

"Hey, baby, is everything ok?" Angie asked.

"Yeah, everything good. I was just checking on you, but where you at?" he asked.

"Me and the girls are at the movies!" Angie said.

"Oh okay. Well, we will see y'all tomorrow, alright baby?" RJ hung up.

"Y'all something ain't right. Them niggas up to something," Angie said, looking at me and Sha.

"Shit, ain't no telling with them, and I don't know why Mel's ass calling me," I said.

We made our way back into the movies. We got closer to the guys and watched the last of the movie. When the movie was over, we met at a restaurant to eat. We all sat together and laughed and joked. When we finished, we walked outside and continued talking.

"Sha, you or Angie can drive. I don't feel like it!" I said.

"I'll drive you home that way you can spend some alone time with me," Real spoke. I took him up on his offer.

It was now 10:30 pm, and we decided to stay and have a drink. Real drove my car with me on the passenger side. El drove his car with Sha, Saun, and Angie.

The ride home was quiet, and I was enjoying every minute with Real.

"So, what y'all want to sip on...Ciroc?" Real teased me. I told him to shut up while I called Sha. I told Sha we were stopping by the store to grab some drinks.

Real

$\mathcal{I}$ was on the phone with El telling him about some lil' crusty lip ass nigga in the store trying to holla at Nel. The dude told Nel he would eat her pussy four different ways. El started laughing. He asked how far I was from Nel's house, and I told him we were pulling up in a few minutes when I heard him say,

"Is that that nigga, Benz?"

"Yes, that's my baby's father," I heard Sha say through the phone.

"You didn't tell me Benz was your baby's father!" El said. I smashed the gas, trying to hurry up and make it there. As soon as we got there, Nel's eyes got big.

"What the hell these niggas doing here?" Nel asked to no one in particular.

I remained calm. I wasn't afraid of them niggas, and I knew Saun was strapped. I saw Mel walking over toward us. He saw me on the driver side, so he swung Nel's door open and grabbed her arm. His hoe ass was looking for a bullet to the head.

"So, bitch, this the shit you do out of spite on a nigga?" Mel yelled at Nel.

"Nigga, let me go. You're hurting my fucking arm!" Nel said, trying to move his hand from around her wrist.

"What this nigga doing driving my shit, and why are you with him?" Mel had the nerve to ask.

"Nigga, this my shit, and you can—"

"Look, I'm gon' say this once, let my girl arm go before I fuck your ass up again," I interrupted Nel.

"Nigga, you ain't gon' do shit just like the last time, bitch ass nigga," Mel said.

Benz was now yelling at Sha, and the tension was much higher.

"You in the car with my connect peoples and shit. What type of shit is this?" Benz said.

"Benz, please calm down!" Sha said.

"Naw, fuck that shit. You better dismiss your boy before I do," Benz said.

Sha didn't want to. You could tell by her eyes. The shit even sounded fucked up. How was she going to look telling El to leave because her baby's daddy said so?

"Okay, you ain't gon' tell this nigga to leave? Alright look, homeboy, if you want no beef with me then I suggest you leave!" Benz said.

El just laughed before talking.

"Look, Benz, I have no problems with you, but she's just your baby's mother, not your girl. If she doesn't want me to leave, then I'm not, and you gon' have to respect that.

Next thing I knew, Benz walked over and punched El right in the face. Saun jumped out with his burner, and I was making my way over. Money pulled his burner out also. Everyone got quiet.

Nel spoke first, "Look this is not necessary. Please, just stop this."

"Naw, Money, shoot that nigga, Real, first!" Mel yelled.

Sha walked in front of El, I guess she was really feeling my nigga.

"Look, Benz, this is stupid tell your boys to back off," Sha said to Benz, standing in front of El. I'm guessing she thought that Benz wouldn't let them shoot at him if she was in the way.

"So, you like this nigga that much you willing to take a bullet for him?" Benz asked Sha.

Sha didn't answer, which pissed Benz off. When she didn't move, Benz took that as a yes.

"Yo, fall back y'all. Let's roll the fuck out this shit. They ain't worth it…none of them," Benz said, walking away.

I could tell Money or Cruz didn't want to withdraw their weapons, but they had to. Benz, Cru, and Money all left. Mel was still behind, and I couldn't understand why.

"Angie, get in your car, and go home. I'll meet you there!" RJ said. Angie just did as he said.

Now, it was Mel, Nel, Sha, El, Saun, and me. Sha talked to El for a minute.

Mel was standing there looking stupid.

"Mel, go home. We're not together anymore. I'm sure Candy and Kim waiting for you!"

Mel's eyes grew wider. He must have not known that Nel knew

that shit.

"Look, Real, I don't know what she told you, but before I left, she was just kissing me and hugging all on a nigga. We trying to work this out. So, if you don't quit sweating my girl, I will put a bullet in your head next time!"

"Mel, are you fucking stupid? We're not together! Please, just leave my house before I call the police," Nel said.

Mel looked at her like he wanted to hurt her. I knew he must've felt embarrassed.

"You know what? When this nigga done selling your ass a dream, you'll be back, and if you're lucky, I might take your ass back." Mel jumped into his ride and drove off. Sha, El and Saun left at the same time, leaving Nel and I alone.

"Hey, I'm so sorry, Real. I don't want you involved in our mess. Maybe we should just end this!"

"What? Because that nigga said so? Hell naw. I'm only gon' stop if that's really what you want, C. Is that what you want?" I asked, hoping she didn't.

"No, it's not, but you guys pulling guns out on each other is also not what I want."

"Look, Nel, I can handle Mel, but I need to know if you want me like I want you!"

She stared at me for what seemed like forever. I raised my eyebrows, wanting to know her answer.

"Real, I like you and I do want to be your girl, but we got to take it slow!"

"I can take it slow or fast…however you want it." I pulled her closer to me.

"I'm serious, Real, be patient with me," she said.

"Can I come in and show you how slow I can take it?" I asked while rubbing her ass.

"What? No, what if Mel comes back?"

"Girl, I'm not worried about his ass, but you could come home with me for the night and have those drinks we bought. Either way you have to take me home," I laughed.

"Okay, let me pack some things first." She walked into her house to grab her things.

I sat in the living room waiting for her to finishing packing her overnight bag so that we could head over to my condo. I never brought a woman to my condo. This was something new to me.

When we made it to my condo, Nel just laughed.

"You stay like five minutes from me. How come I didn't know that?" she asked.

"I told you I live close. That's how I seen you and ol' boy hugging and shit!"

We walked into my condo. She mentioned that my shit was much bigger and nicer than hers, even though her shit was nice also.

"It's so nice. Did your mother decorate for you?" Nel asked. I know she really wanted to know if another bitch decorated my shit.

"Yes, my mother did help. You should see her house, though."

We got comfortable and cuddled on the couch. It felt so good having her in my arms. She started kissing me, and I kissed her back.

"So, you want it slow, right?" I asked, pulling down her pants.

"Yes, please," she said as she started unbuttoning my shirt.

We had sex for about an hour before we showered and did it again. We laid in my bed and fell asleep.

I was waking up when I overheard Nel talking on the phone. Her phone volume was so loud I could hear everything Angie and Sha was asking her. Women love being on three-way.

"Girl, you okay?" Angie and Sha asked.

"Girl, yeah. Mel's ass is crazy. He was just showing out as usual, but I didn't want to stay home, so I'm at Real's house," Nel told the girls.

"Damn, I guess you are over Mel?" Angie laughed.

"Girl, like never before! I'll call y'all tomorrow, though. I'm so tired. This drama shit needs to end!" Nel said.

"Girl, who you telling? Benz been blowing my cell phone up all damn night. Them niggas flew here and left Money's car there just so they could see what the fuck we were doing," Sha laughed.

"Yeah, I wonder how they found out," Nel said.

"That dude that was mugging Real at the movies on the way in," Angie told them.

"So, you and RJ good?" Sha asked Angie.

"I don't know. He hasn't said anything to me since we got home. He's in the guest room now."

"Damn, well let me call Benz back so he can stop calling," Sha said, hanging up. I pretended to still be asleep while Nel laid her head on my chest.

Sha

I called Benz because I wanted to get the shit out the way.

"Hello!" Benz answered with much attitude.

"You the one blowing up my damn phone, so gon' with that shit!" I said.

"Where you at?" he asked.

"I'm at home. Why?"

"Open the door then!"

He hung up and sure enough, when I checked outside, he was out there. *This nigga is a stalker*! I thought to myself.

Benz walked in and took his shoes off like he was staying or something.

"Why is you taking your shit off? You can't stay here, Benz!" I said.

"Why? Your little boyfriend coming over later tonight? No. Fuck that. Daddy's home now," he smirked.

I couldn't deal with his ass. I just went in my room and shut my door.

Why do I let him do this to me? I finally find a nigga I like, and his ass making shit so hard for me. I thought to myself.

Knock. Knock.

"What, Benz?" I asked, wishing he would just leave.

"Can I come in?"

"Yeah!" I sighed, knowing if I said no, he would come in anyway.

"Sha, can we talk? Because you owe me an explanation."

"I don't owe you shit, but we can talk about why you didn't bring my son like you were supposed to!"

"My sitter bringing him tomorrow morning, and you do owe me something. Why you fucking with that nigga, El? I thought we were working on us getting back together?"

"Benz, I never said that. You did!"

"So, you telling me you want to have something with that nigga?"

"Yes, I do, Benz!" Benz was quiet. I knew him all too well. He was hurting, but oh fucking well.

"Okay. I don't like it and just so you know, that nigga better not be around my son," he said.

He knew exactly what he was doing. Benz knew if I couldn't bring Junior around El, it would be hard to be with him. I just sat there. Benz was sitting on my bed looking sexy as always. I did want to fix things between us in the past, but I liked El and wanted to see how things would go.

"Okay, can you leave now?" I said.

"No, I can't, but let me get some of my pussy, and you better not give my pussy away?"

Benz didn't need me to say anything, my face said it all.

"So, you letting that nigga hit my pussy, Sha?" Benz said, looking into my eyes. "Sha, you fucking this nigga?" he asked again.

I never answered him, and he walked out of my room and my house. I ran after him, but it was too late. I didn't want him to do anything stupid.

"Benz, please, let me explain. I didn't want things to end up like this!" Benz turned around and looked into my eyes.

"You knew that I wanted to fix our relationship for our son. When he asks why we can't all live together and be a family, you gon' be the one to tell him why. Oh, I'm moving down here on Monday. My movers already got my shit loaded. I guess I'll be looking for a crib since you got a man and shit."

Benz was hurt. I could see it in his eyes, but he waited too long to try to get me back. He had been replaced.

Nel

A month went by, and things were somewhat back to normal. I was back at work and busy with school. Real and I became an official couple. Mel has been missing in action. I haven't heard from him in a while, not that I wanted to anyway.

Angie made up with RJ. Although she spent some days chilling with Saun, nothing was going down between them. I told her she needed to end that lil' shit with Saun. I wasn't a fan of that cheating shit.

Sha had her son home, and she was happy she spent the last two weeks catching up with him. Benz had moved to Chicago, so he could be closer to them. He tried everything to get Sha back. Sha was still kicking it with El, but they haven't put a title on what they were. I told her to just ask him, no use in sitting around wondering if she was his girl or not.

I was just getting ready to get off work. It's was a long and stressful day. All I wanted to do was go home. Real had to handle some business in the street earlier, so he couldn't take me to lunch on my break like he's done for the past week.

Every day on my break, he would pick me up and take me to lunch, and I really felt like the queen. Although we weren't staying together, I spent a lot of time at his house. He bought me a whole new wardrobe just for his place.

I decided to just go home. I haven't been home in a few days. I've just stopped by to check the mail.

When I got home, I took off my heels. My feet were hurting so bad. I decided on a quick shower before I had to study for my test tomorrow. After I showered, I fired up my computer and went through my notes. My phone was vibrating on the table, so I ignored it and kept going through my notes for a good hour. When I finally finished, I checked my phone. Real had called me twice. I called him back right away.

"Hey, baby. What's up?" I asked Real.

"Nothing, baby. I've called you twice. What's up? You still mad I couldn't take you to lunch?" he asked.

"No, I was never mad, and I was studying for my test tomorrow morning."

"Oh cool, so are you still studying?" he asked, sounding sexy.

"No, I'm done now. I'm just relaxing because I'm tired. Wednesdays are really busy days at work," I said.

"Oh, so I take it you're not coming over tonight?"

"No, I'm gon' stay home tonight. I got to be up at eight o'clock to take my test." I said as I stretched out on my couch.

"Come on, baby. Well, do you want me to come over?" he asked.

"No, it's okay. Besides, you'll keep me up all night!"

"Alright, baby. Call me later before you head to bed. I'm gon' head over to El's since you're not messing with me tonight."

"Real, it's not even like that. I'm just tired. I'll call you later, baby."

"Yeah, okay, sexy."

We ended the call, and I turned my TV on.

Mel

I was leaving the hospital. It's been weeks since I heard from my boys or Nel. They all knew my mom was sick, but no one knew she was getting ready to die. I felt empty and lost without my girl, and now I was losing my mom. I thought about the time I brought Nel over to meet my mom. Nel was so nervous she wouldn't get out of the car. I assured her that it would be okay, and it went great. My mom, Cathy, loved Nel the first time she met her. They became good friends. My mom treated Nel like the daughter she never had, and Nel loved her dearly. I dropped a tear thinking about it. I knew it was my fault that Nel left, and I wished I could change it all. I decided to hit the fellows up. I hadn't talked to Benz in days.

"Yo, Benz, what up?" I said through the phone.

"What's good with you? Ain't heard from your ass. How your mom doing?" Benz asked.

"She holding on. They gave her a week at the most to live. I just left there, and she look so bad, man. I couldn't stay long. I hate to see her like that!"

"Damn, Mel. Why you ain't tell me? You know I would have come up there with you."

"I know, man. I just didn't know how to deal with the shit!"

"Man, I know it hurts, and I can't say I know how you feel, but I'm here for you, man, on some real shit!"

"Thanks, bro. I appreciate that. You busy, though? I'm about to grab a drink. Can I come through?"

"I'm not doing shit. Junior's ass just went to sleep, but come on through. I got that good shit we can smoke, and I'll hit RJ and Money up too!" he mentioned.

"Cool, I'll be there in twenty." I hung up and headed toward the corner liquor store before heading over to Benz's house.

Sha

I was sitting on the couch with El. I just got out of class, so I stopped over. I had a test tomorrow and was confident I would do great.

"Hey, baby, I think I'm going to head home in a minute," I said, looking at the clock.

"No, I want you here with me tonight, baby. I need some loving. You been holding out on a nigga!" El said as he tried grabbing my breasts.

"I have not. I've just been tired, but I got a test tomorrow, and the school is closer to my house."

"Ugh, I guess, but what you doing tomorrow? Maybe I can take you and Junior out to eat?"

El met Junior once, and that was by accident when he bumped into us coming from the sandwich shop. I never properly introduced them, so El introduced himself to my little man. I didn't want to start anything between El and Benz, so I never brought Junior around El because Benz didn't want our son around him.

"Um, I don't know. He might be with his dad tomorrow." I said as I gathered my stuff to leave.

"What? I thought you said you were getting him tomorrow? You lying to me, Sha-Sha?"

"No, Benz just asked can he take him somewhere…that's all," I lied not wanting to tell him he wasn't allowed to see my son.

"Oh, okay. Well, we're getting real close. I just want to get to know him," El grabbed me by my waist.

"Okay, baby. I'll see what I can do."

I was getting ready to leave when Real walked in.

"Hey, homeboy, where my girl at?" I asked.

"She at home. She ain't fucking with your boy tonight!" Real said.

"Damn, something in the air because Sha's ass leaving me tonight too," El added.

"What y'all got up?" El asked.

"Nothing. We both got tests in the morning and if you know us, we don't play when it comes down to that education, baby," I hugged El and left.

I haven't talked to my son all day, so I called him. I waited on the phone until Benz picked up.

"What?"

That was his first response when he answered. I had to look at the phone to make sure it was the right person.

"Hey, I was calling checking on Junior. What is your problem?" I asked.

Benz had been acting really funny with me I knew why; I just didn't feed into his bullshit.

"He's asleep, and I don't have a problem. You picked a fine time to call him. You been with your boy all day?" he asked.

"So, that's why you throwing shade my way? Benz, let that shit go. We supposed to be good for our son, and you making it hard for me!"

"Yeah, and we supposed to be a family, but you too busy dick hopping that you can't make that happen!"

I couldn't believe he said dick hopping. That was a blow way below the belt. He knew I wasn't that type of girl. El was the first guy I've been with sexually in a long time.

"Have him call me tomorrow!" I didn't even let him respond before I hung up.

Benz

I knew I shouldn't have said that about dick hoping, but I was still pissed about Sha being with El. The beef between us men didn't stop the crew from making money, we all had the same motto and that was getting money. We would make money and feed our family before beefing with each other in the street. I wanted to call her and apologize, but I felt like it wouldn't matter. I heard the fellows coming in the door so I got up to greet them.

"Yo', nigga, I hope you got some food in here a nigga hungry as fuck!" Money said coming in first.

"Nigga, you always hungry, but yeah, it's some steak and potatoes on the stove," I said as I greeted Mel and RJ.

They made their way into the living room. My house was nice. I had six bedrooms with four bathrooms, the basement was furnished with two additional rooms that I planned to make into an exercise room.

"Which one of y'all niggas wants to get y'all asses whooped in this game first?" I asked, turning the game on.

"Shit, I guess I will since these niggas scared!" RJ said.

I never lost a game when we played Madden NFL 25. That's why I always wanted to play it. But when it came to Call of Duty: Black Ops, RJ won most of the time.

We played the game for over three hours and Mel was drunk, I told him to crash at my crib tonight. Everyone else made their way home. I checked on Jr. and he was still sleeping as he sucked his thumb, I hated when he did that, but it helps his little butt sleep.

I jumped into the shower and went to my room across from my son's room. I wanted Junior to live with me permanently, but Sha thought that since we were beefing, it would be better if Junior just stayed with her.

I remembered when I first met Sha. I asked Angie who she was. I thought Nel was cute, but Sha had way more ass than her at the time. So, when I got her, I treated her like a queen. When I got caught up in the streets, I didn't know how to balance that life with priorities with Sha being my number one focus. I didn't get it until Sha had Junior and even then, I was still fucking up. When Sha left, it took me two years to finally give it all up, but what do I have to show for it? My family was broken and when I came back to claim what was mine, Sha was already in too deep with another nigga, especially by giving my pussy up.

I hated that she did that and it hurt like hell, but I was gon' still try every chance I got to get her back. I was interrupted from my thoughts by Junior talking in his sleep. I laughed because he was always doing that.

Angie

I was sitting on my couch, looking out the window and talking to Saun. I was watching out because RJ called and said he was on his way home. I wasn't necessarily cheating on him because I felt like if I didn't sleep with Saun, I wasn't cheating on RJ.

I saw RJ pull up, so I hurried up and got off the phone with Saun. I didn't really like him enough to leave RJ. I just liked talking to him. He was easy to talk to, and he made me laugh. Saun wanted me bad, all he talked about was fucking me.

I opened the door for RJ. "Hey, baby, I missed you!" I said and hugged him tight.

"I missed you too. I missed that pussy even more. You gon' take care of daddy tonight?" RJ kissed my neck.

I knew I had to, or he would start to question me about not having sex on the regular like we used to. I wanted to, but I was getting bored with him. Nel said that was because someone else was entertaining me other than RJ. We walked upstairs, and RJ removed all of my clothes. He massaged my back until he started to rub my booty and he kissed it. He opened my legs wider and started kissing my pussy from the back. He was a pro when it came to sucking my pussy. It was the dick game that was boring me. I was coming, and RJ sucked all my juices out of me. I just hoped the dick game was just as good. I rode RJ and made him come. I started imagining him to be Saun, and I was cumming all over his dick. We cuddled for a bit, and RJ left. I was excited for the weekend.

I knew I was wrong for thinking about Saun while having sex with RJ, but I just needed that fire again or something to spice up our relationship. It didn't hurt to fantasize a little. I was in love with RJ and couldn't wait to start a family with him, but we needed to spice it up a bit.

Mel

I was sitting at home when I got a phone call telling me to come to the hospital, the doctors gave my mom a week to live, but she held on for two more weeks. I was more content in the fact she had passed. In a way, I was happy that she wasn't suffering anymore, but it hurt like hell, and I felt all alone. I wanted many times to reach out and tell Nel, but I decided to leave her alone. She had a man now, and I didn't want to bother her with my problems.

I got to the hospital and my uncle, aunt, and my crew was there to support me besides them, I had no one. After seeing my mom, the doctors gave me all the information I would need. Her funeral arrangements had already been made. It was Wednesday, and she would get buried Friday. I left the hospital and my aunt, uncle, and my boys came to my house with food.

Some of the people from the church my mom attended had stopped by to give their condolences.

"Jamel, you have been so strong through this rough time, and I want you to know that your mother will always be with you. She doesn't want you crying and stressing yourself, baby, so please take care of yourself. Your uncle and I will be here if you need us, but we're going to head home," my aunt said.

I didn't have words for her, so I just hugged her tight. It made me feel so good to know she was here with me. I couldn't hold the tears back.

"It's okay, baby. Get it all out. Crying is good, baby. It's the next step to healing, baby," she said.

I hugged my aunt tighter. I didn't know if I would have made it without her.

"Thanks, Auntie, for being here and helping me. I love you for that," I told her.

My mom and aunt didn't get along, but she told me she wasn't about to have me dealing with all of this alone. Benz walked up and hugged me. It was good having someone in my corner. As everyone came in and out for what seem like forever. I was finally able to rest my head.

Sha

I couldn't believe my ears. I called Benz to get Junior, but he was with Mel. He told me that Mel's mom died. I thought that she was doing well with chemotherapy. I called Nel so she could know.

"Hey, Nel. Can you talk?" I asked Nel when she picked up the phone.

"Yes. What's good, boo?" Nel said not hearing the seriousness in my voice.

"Nel, I talked to Benz, and he told me Mel's mom died earlier today." It was quiet for a good minute.

"Nel, you there?" I said into the phone.

"Sha, are you serious? Why didn't anyone tell me she was that sick. I would've been there with him dealing with that. OMG!"

"I know, but just call him. He probably needs you right now, and you were close to his mom, so I know he needs your support!"

"You're right. I'll stop by there in a minute."

We talked for a while longer. Nel felt so bad she couldn't believe he didn't even tell her his mom wasn't doing well with chemo. She said she had to go over there and see him.

Nel

I was in the living room when Real came in from the basement.

"What's wrong, baby? It looks like you lost your best friend."

"Real, I got to run over to Angie's something happened, and she's crying, so I'll be back shortly!"

I was already running out the house. I didn't want Real to ask if I wanted him to go. I called Mel's phone, but he didn't answer. *What if he's having crazy thoughts? He always said if something happened to his mom he would go crazy.*

When I got to what use to be our house, I noticed his car outside. I knocked on the door, and I stood outside for five minutes, and he still didn't come to the door. I wondered if he still had the spare key in the garage under his tool box. I opened his car door and was happy that he didn't lock his doors. I hit the garage opener. I went in found the spare key where I knew it would be.

When I got in the house, I put my purse and cell phone on the counter in walked in his room. I heard him crying, and my heart just dropped. I couldn't believe he had to go through this.

"Mel?" I said as I tried not to startle him.

He raised his head up and looked at me.

"Nel, what are you doing here?"

He seemed shocked that I was in his house standing in his bedroom.

"Mel, why didn't you tell me about Cathy? You know I cared about her."

"I'm sorry, Nel. I meant to, but things just happened so fast. I figured you didn't want to be bothered with that!"

He was starting to cry now. If anyone understood how much he loved and cared about his mom, it would be me.

"Shhh! Mel, it's okay, baby, just let it out," I tried comforting him.

He may have hurt me, but I wouldn't wish this pain on my worst enemy. It was quiet, and I held Mel for about an hour.

"Mel, I got to get home. Are you going to be okay?"

"No, Nel, please don't leave me. I need you tonight. Nel, please, I can't lie here and deal with this by myself. Please stay. I promise I won't try anything!"

I decided to stay. I would have to think of something to tell Real, but the truth wouldn't make sense to him. Mel was drifting off to sleep, but every now and then he would open his eyes and make sure I was there. He pulled me closer.

"Nel, please, let me make love to you. I need you to ease my mind," Mel said, bringing his lips to mine. I moved back, but he wouldn't let me go. His lip got closer to mine.

"Please Nel, that's all I need." I felt torn, but I knew what I had to do.

Real

I had been calling Nel's phone for about an hour now. I was getting pissed and worried at the same time. I called Sha and Angie, but they haven't seen her. Angie seemed like she had more to say, but I knew how that sister code shit worked. I didn't mention anything about what Nel told me about her crying. I felt like it wasn't my business. I sat on the couch thinking that maybe she was at home studying.

I got up and decided to see if she was at home. When I got there, her car wasn't in the driveway, so I thought it could've been in the garage. I rang the doorbell, but she never answered. I couldn't think of where she could be. She just started her last classes on campus, but she didn't have class today. I tried calling her phone again, but I still got the voicemail.

"Man, what the fuck? God, please let my baby be okay!" I said out loud.

I walked back to my car. I drove home to see if she made it back there, hoping maybe her phone was dead and couldn't get in touch with me. I made it home in record time, it usually took me five minutes to get from my condo to hers, and I made it there in two minutes. I tried to just let it go, but I couldn't. Something in my gut told me something was up.

I hit up my private investigator that I kept on payroll for my personal and street business.

"Aye, Clint, I got a job for you," I said into the phone.

"Aye, long time no hear, and what might that job be?" Clint asked.

"I need you to look up a Jamel and find out where he lay his head. When you find him, I need you to see if a female is there. Better yet, meet me at the spot, and I'll give you more details!"

I was about to see if my gut feeling was telling me what I would hate to think. I met with Clint at our spot. I showed him a picture of Nel and Nel's car.

"Yo, Clint, I need that shit ASAP, man, ASAP," I told Clint, getting ready to go.

"I got you, man. Have I ever let you down?" he asked and smiled.

"No, I can't say that you have. Get with me soon!" I said, walking off.

I left and went home. I smoked a blunt to ease my mind. I played my PS4 and finally laid down. I wasn't going to sleep, but I was tired. Three hours went by. I was just about to close my eyes my phone started to ring.

"Clint, tell me you found something?" I said.

"Oh, yes indeed, my man! Okay, here it goes. I found this Jamel cat. It wasn't hard since he's the only one with that name in this area, but I got some pictures for you that you may want to see. I'm one hundred percent sure that the picture you showed me earlier is the girl in the pictures I took a while ago."

I was hurt I never thought I could feel this way again. I gave Nel my heart. I thought it may have been too soon, but she assured me she really cared for me.

"Alright, I'm on my way!" I said.

I drove as fast as I could to our meeting spot. When I made it inside, Clint had the pictures spread across a table. I couldn't believe the shit I was seeing. There she was hugged up in bed with Mel. All the pics were basically the same, her holding him as if she was consoling him, but the last picture stopped my heart. I paid Clint for his service and went home with my evidence. I didn't know if she was coming back or just leaving me hanging.

Nel

I woke up, and it was very late I knew I needed to go home, but I wanted to be there for Mel. I hated that I had to lie to Real, but he wouldn't understand why I had to be there for Mel. I looked at my phone, and it was dead. I grabbed Mel's charger and charged my phone. I knew Real called and was probably worried. I decided that I would have to leave Mel tonight to go home and explain to Real.

"Mel, I'm leaving, it's really late, but I'll come and check on you tomorrow, okay?"

Mel open his eyes. He told me it was the first time he actually got some good sleep.

"Nel, please, I need you. I need you home with me. Fuck that nigga. He just using you to get to me!"

I knew that wasn't true, but I had to get home.

"Look, Mel, I'll call and check on you tomorrow. I can't stay. Please don't argue with me on this. You need to be taking care of yourself. Don't worry about the unnecessary!

"So, you're just going to leave like that?" he asked.

"Mel, I already crossed the line. I am in a relationship now. I shouldn't have did what I did in the first place."

"I'm not trying to hear all that shit. What? You trying to be loyal to that nigga? Whatever, Nel. I'm good!" he said, getting out the bed and entering the bathroom.

I just looked at him. It was hard leaving him knowing what he'd been through.

"You can let yourself out. I'll holler at you!" he yelled from the bathroom.

I left. I felt bad. I thought maybe it was because I still cared for him, but truth is, I thought he needed someone. I knew how much he loved his mom. I didn't want to go back to Real's, but I wanted to get it over with. It was getting very late, and I called off work because I knew it would be a long night. My co-worker understood that I needed time off. They gave me the rest of the week off to grieve for who they assumed to be my mother-in-law. I didn't correct them and say I wasn't with Mel anymore.

I got to Real's house, and I felt my heart racing. I put my key in the hole and turned the knob. The living room was dark, but the light from the kitchen shed a little light in the hallway.

I called Real's name, but he didn't answer. I reached over and turned on the lights, and he was sitting on his favorite chair, looking at me like he wanted me dead.

"Real, you scared me, baby. Didn't you hear me calling you?" I asked, but he just stared at me. "Real, I know I didn't answer my phone, but let me explain."

He didn't respond. He just threw a manila envelope on the table. I looked at it and back at him.

"What's that?" I asked.

"Open it. It's a surprise for you!" he said with a smirk.

I walked over to where he was sitting and sat down. I opened the envelope and felt my heart jump out of my chest. There were pictures of me and Mel. The next picture is what took my breath away.

"So, I guess you don't have to waste your time making up a lie now, do you?"

What could I say? The evidence sat there looking right at me.

TO BE CONTINUED

Looking for a publishing home?

Royalty Publishing House, Where the Royals reside, is accepting submissions for writers in the urban fiction genre. If you're interested, submit the first 3-4 chapters with your synopsis to submissions@royaltypublishinghouse.com.

Check out our website for more information: www.royaltypublishinghouse.com.

Do You Like CELEBRITY GOSSIP?

Check Out QUEEN DYNASTY!
Visit Our Site: www.thequeendynasty.com

Get LiT!

Download the LiT eReader app today and enjoy exclusive

content, free books, and more

CPSIA information can be obtained
at www.ICGtesting.com
Printed in the USA
LVOW13s2120190417
531410LV00014B/278/P